NILAY'S WISH

By Riya Aarini

Illustrated by Akos Horvath

Nilay's Wish
Text copyright © 2019 by Riya Aarini. Illustrations copyright © 2019 by Akos Horvath

ISBN 978-1-7331661-1-9

Book design by Author Packages
Author photograph by Sally Blood

Publisher's Cataloging-in-Publication Data
provided by Five Rainbows Cataloging Services

Names: Aarini, Riya, author. | Horvath, Akos, illustrator.
Title: Nilay's wish / by Riya Aarini ; illustrated by Akos Horvath.
Description: Chicago : Riya Aarini, 2019. | Summary: Nilay releases the apprentice genie Jai and finds himself in historical India on a quest for the perfect red silk saree. | Audience: Grades 3-6.
Identifiers: LCCN 2019909009 (print) | ISBN 978-1-7331661-0-2 (paperback) | ISBN 978-1-7331661-1-9 (hardcover) | ISBN 978-1-7331661-2-6 (ebook) | ISBN 978-1-7331661-3-3 (audiobook)
Subjects: LCSH: Jinn--Juvenile fiction. | Children's stories. | CYAC: Genies--Fiction. | Friendship--Fiction. | India--Fiction. | Adventure and adventurers--Fiction. | BISAC: JUVENILE FICTION / Historical / Asia. | JUVENILE FICTION / Action & Adventure / General. | JUVENILE FICTION / Social Themes / Friendship.
Classification: LCC PZ7.1.A27 Ni 2019 (print) | LCC PZ7.1.A27 (ebook) | DDC [Fic]--dc23.

To my mom and brother,
some of the kindest people to ever grace the planet

Find true friendship in adversity.

Discover courage in the grips of fear.

Know yourself in the midst of the unknown.

Contents

Preface

The artisans of India are a dynamic source of inspiration both today and in times long gone. These imaginative artists take bits of absolutely nothing and create stunning somethings that translate into incredible works of art.

Saurashtrian silk weavers are included in this timeless category of artisans. With a simple handloom, some silk thread and a mat on the floor, these illustrious weavers create rich, enduring art. Here is a glimpse into their story.

Chapter 1
A Surprise Friend

NILAY PEERED CURIOUSLY AT the brass lamp, which shone like a glimmering yellow sapphire under the midmorning sun. He cradled the lamp perfectly in his small hands. Strangely enough, the lamp curled at the tip, like an elephant's trunk when it thirstily sprays water into its mouth.

The inviting breeze at the Toronto park had drawn Nilay and his mom and dad out for a beachside excursion. Canada had balmy days, and today was one of them. Nilay glanced up into the blue sky, where a mystical haze played peek-a-boo with the sun. Flying seagulls squawked. Lake Ontario's waves tossed against the rocks upon which Nilay crouched. Turning his head, he refocused his attention on the dazzling antique he had discovered concealed between the rocks.

The boy had seen the golden sparkle from a distance at the edge of the beach. The gold drew him, as if beckoning. Usually,

Nilay stayed away from the water, as he had not yet picked up swimming. His last experience with deep water was when he had slipped off a lake rock, smoothed by decades of waves. He had nearly drowned before his dad pulled him ashore.

The recent misfortune instilled in him a sense of fear of water's unknown depths. His parents promptly scheduled swim lessons, but Nilay was not ready. He knew he had to learn how to swim to overcome his trepidation of bottomless waters. But for the time being, lakes and rivers appeared spectacular only from afar.

This time at the beach was different, though. He could not understand why. The lamp poking out from between the rocks exuded an aura of security, like a haven. Nilay, overwhelmed with feelings of safety, had cautiously approached the antique, carefully stepping from rock to rock before quickly grasping the lamp sandwiched between the pointy shards jutting out from the lake's increasing depth. That was how he got ahold of it. Now it was in his possession.

Back at the rock-strewn shoreline, Nilay's reflection shone in the lamp. One teensy spot was a blur, so the young boy took the edge of his T-shirt and rubbed the fuzzy area.

"Ah! Now the lamp is perfect!" Nilay proudly whispered to himself. He had a tendency to do things as perfectly as could be. At the same time, his gracious nature welcomed flaws with open arms. The boy's adaptability had served him well throughout his eleven years of life. In this particular moment, though, Nilay leaned toward his perfectionist side. "Brass should shine!" he said.

Just then, the lamp shook and shimmered! It flipped from Nilay's hands like a goldfish out of water and landed on the rocks.

Nilay stared in awe at the gleaming object.

A wisp of smoke streamed out of the tippity-top of the lamp. The wisp grew into a tuft of smoke, then a cloud, then....

"At your service, Master!" chirped a squeaky voice.

Nilay's eyes widened as he stared in disbelief at the youth in front of him.

In sheer astonishment, Nilay managed to utter a few words.

"Are...are you...a genie?"

"Well, technically, no," said the boy. "You could say I'm a genie-in-training. My dad, he's the real genie. He's in the kitchen cooking up his usual *amazing* lunch. You know, flat breads stuffed with chopped onions and oodles of goat cheese, lots of steaming rice and freshly fried samosas...my favorite of all favorites! Lunch promises to be better than a daydream. I can't wait to dig in. You know, Dad always whips together the most delicious spread!"

Nilay gulped. He started to feel hungry, too.

"What's the matter?" asked the apprentice genie.

"I...I..." mumbled Nilay. The boy glanced downward. His shyness overcame him.

"I'm Jai," said the little genie with a wide grin.

"I...I'm Nilay. I'm eleven years old."

"Eleven? Me, too! Well, if you add a couple zeros!" said Jai, holding his belly and laughing heartily.

After a couple seconds of thought, Nilay, in astonishment, asked, "You're eleven hundred years old?"

"Yep! I know, I'm young. But my dad, he's eleven hundred thousand years old. He says he'll live forever."

Nilay was dumbstruck. He could hardly imagine even a million years.

The young genie started chatting about his years in the

lamp, about the drastic weather inside, the hot, the cold, the rainy mornings and the mosquitoes, the scrumptious food his dad cooked up when he was in a good mood and the horrible boredom when no one rubbed the lamp....

Nilay rubbed his eyes. He pinched his arm to make sure he wasn't dreaming. He had lived his entire life in Toronto and had never witnessed a spellbinding event like this.

"So," said Jai, "what's your wish?"

The genie-in-training stood in front of Nilay with his purple arms on his hips and a comical grin on his face. Jai, decked in a stunning gold vest, coolly rubbed his fingers on his chest and blew into them.

"I...I...get a...wish?" stuttered Nilay.

"Of course! You rubbed the lamp, right? I've got a few tricks to learn. But since I'm filling in for Dad for a bit, at least until lunch, I can attempt to grant any wish you desire!" said Jai.

"Right, of course. I did rub the lamp, and you are a magical genie, and I'm not dreaming, and..."

"Go on...go on," said Jai, smiling. "As a genie apprentice, I am eager to fulfill my very first wish!"

"Well," thought Nilay out loud, as his brown eyes looked up at the sky. He rubbed his chin. "My mom's birthday is today. I haven't found the perfect gift yet. She always says I'm her present, but still, I'd like to get her a really, *really* nice gift."

"You're getting closer!" said Jai, grinning and rubbing his hands together.

"Mom loves red...and she..." said Nilay, still in deep thought.

"Yeeessss?" said Jai. The genie's voice crescendoed with excitement.

"...She's always smiling when she wears anything made of

silk," continued Nilay.

"Mmmm…hmmm!"

"I wish…I wish for the most perfect red silk saree in the world!" blurted Nilay, his eyes tightly shut.

"Granted!" said Jai, smiling.

"Huh?" replied Nilay, his eyes popping open, as if he'd just stumbled out of a trance.

"Okay, we've got to get things moving," Jai said, busily looking around and scratching his head. "I like to do things a little differently as a young genie, you know."

"What do you mean?" asked Nilay.

"My dad, the real genie, could promptly fulfill your wish for the best silk saree in the world. So can I—but I want to kick wish-granting up a notch. Are you in?"

"That sounds cool," said Nilay, finding instant comfort in his new genie friend. "What do you have in mind?"

"Well, picture this." Jai put on a film director's cap he whipped out of thin air. "Instead of dropping the world's best red silk saree into your hands this second, I want to take you back to when and where weaving silk sarees got its fine start. You'll see firsthand the culture, the people and the history."

Nilay's eyes widened like two porcelain dinner plates. He loved history. The bookshelf in his bedroom was evidence of his fondness for all things historical. Sitting on the shelves were a huge atlas of the world, dozens of colorful books about the cultures of various countries and a globe—even though finding a globe in a boy's room these days was a rarity.

Nilay warmed up to Jai's idea fast. He cracked a smile. An adventure *and* a peek into history promised to be too splendid for the boy to resist. Giddy with excitement, he nodded emphatically in agreement.

"A trek into the unknown!" shrieked Nilay with the zeal

of an explorer on a quest for a treasure. To him, visiting antiquity was a mystery only half revealed in history books.

Jai, with a cheery grin on his face, said, "That's right! Shouldn't take long. We'll be back by lunchtime!"

Nilay, mingling the bravado of youth and the daring of an adventurer, boldly proclaimed, "Let's do this!"

The genie pounded his chest once, pointed his index finger to the sky and said, "I may be a novice genie, but let it be known that *newbies* do it best!"

Lake Ontario's waves splashed up against the rocks. A gentle, cool breeze circled around Nilay.

Jai held out his hand. Nilay grasped it in a sign of solidarity and friendship. The two instantly vanished in a speckled swirl of colored smoke.

Chapter 2

The Bumpy Landing

"OUCH!" SAID NILAY.

Nilay and Jai both landed with a mild thud on a light dirt mound.

"We're heeere!" squealed Jai. "Your scrunched face and knitted brows speak volumes! Sorry about the rough landing, my friend and master. It's my first time piloting a wish, you know!"

"It's okay," said Nilay as he dusted himself off. "Where are…?"

Before he could finish, a sudden sensation in Nilay's back pocket prompted him to whirl around. "Hey! That's my smartphone!"

The monkey ran a few feet with Nilay's device, staring back at the young boy and genie as if to dare the two.

"That monkey stole my phone!" yelled Nilay. The

excitement provoked by wild monkeys was new to Nilay, as he'd never seen such happenings in the neighborhoods of Toronto.

Jai explained, "In India, monkey mischief is a common occurrence. The animals confiscate anything, like necklaces or hairpieces, in exchange for a delicious morsel. Monkey rowdiness, no matter how illicit, is how the animals earn their living, my friend!"

Nilay chased after the guilty monkey across the dirt mound.

"Oh boy," said Jai, rolling his eyes. "I'll handle this." Jai whipped a banana out of thin air. "Here, use this: the world's most perfect monkey bribe."

Nilay grabbed the banana and enticed the monkey with it. "Come on, you little thief! Let's trade!"

The scrawny monkey edged toward Nilay. The animal put out one hand to grab the banana.

"No, no!" said Nilay. "Not until I get my phone back!" Nilay dangled the banana once again. The monkey dropped the phone, grabbed the banana and scampered off into the distance. Nilay tucked his phone safely back into his pocket.

"Well, there you have it: life in India," said Jai.

"INDIA!" shrieked Nilay. "That's where we are?" Nilay had never stepped out of Canada.

"Why, yes, my friend and master. Where else can we find the finest silk sarees? Specifically, we are in Saurashtra, the original home of the respected silk weavers."

"Wow!" said Nilay.

"Even more specifically, we're in the year 300 CE."

Nilay's jaw dropped. It took a moment for him to digest their travel back in time.

"Saur...?" asked Nilay, as he attempted to pronounce the

region's name.

"Yes, my friend! 'Saur' as in sour cream, sauerkraut, sour pickles," said Jai.

Nilay arched one eyebrow. "Okay, I got it. I got it. Saur...."

"Then 'ashtra,'" said Jai.

"'Ashtra.'"

"Now put it all together like an orchestra playing a symphony!" said Jai, waving his arms in the flamboyant style of a conductor.

"Saurashtra!" said Nilay with a burst of pride.

"Now that's music to my ears!" said Jai.

Pleased with himself, Nilay got comfortable and sat down on the ground. Jai followed his example. Looking at the vastness surrounding him, Nilay asked, "Where is this Saurashtra place?"

"Saurashtra was hardly a blip on a map! For centuries, Saurashtra was its own kingdom, until its rulers were defeated and the region merged with its neighbor. Let me give you a little geography lesson, my friend."

Jai plucked a pair of professorial eyeglasses out of thin air and placed them on the tip of his nose. "In this cultured land of India is this peninsular region known as Saurashtra, near present-day Gujarat. The Arabian sea borders Saurashtra along the south and southwest."

Nilay, a history buff and an avid reader of maps both ancient and contemporary, pictured Gujarat's location. "Saurashtra is on the northwestern coast of India!"

"Right you are!" said Jai. Pushing his eyeglasses toward the bridge of his nose, Jai continued, "In this golden age, Saurashtra is under the magnificent Gupta Empire. Golden fields of rice, copper wheat fields and majestic cotton plants grow on Saurashtra's fertile grounds."

A light clunk on Nilay's head startled him. "Oh no, not another surprise visit from a monkey." Nilay looked up. The shiny, green leaves of the date palm fanned out above him; bunches of fruit hung from the center of the palm. A few dates had fallen to the ground.

"Oh, I forgot to mention. Dates grow in Saurashtra, too," said Jai.

Nilay picked up a date and chomped on it. "Pretty sweet!" He gathered a few more pieces of the fallen fruit and stuffed them into his pockets.

"Go on, Jai," said Nilay, chewing the dates.

"As I was saying," continued Jai, "on our quest for the perfect red silk saree, we've traveled back in time about seventeen hundred years...I think. I'm not a numbers genie myself. Crunching numbers is double duty...."

The wind started to pick up. Surrounded by fertile grounds spotted with rows and rows of date palms, Nilay looked far into the distance. Along the horizon, clusters of farmers' thatched huts appeared like flecks.

The unfamiliar setting appeared secluded to a boy who'd never set foot on a farm, let alone an expansive orchard. Getting fidgety, Nilay said, "I can see these date palms for miles! Are there no people around?"

"My friend and master, especially in ancient times like these, India is one of the most populated civilizations the world has ever known!"

"By the looks of this place, I'd say the population is short about three million," said Nilay. Hailing from Toronto, Nilay was accustomed to crowds and the bustle of big city life.

"We clearly landed in a rural orchard of sorts, with nothing but flourishing date palms! If we're on a search for the perfect red silk saree, we certainly won't find it here growing on trees!" said Jai.

Nilay let out a burst of laughter. He was relieved his new genie friend displayed enough common sense to whisk them out of their predicament.

"I do admit, as a newbie genie, I believe I've navigated to what looks like the wrong spot," said Jai. "Let's go into town, where the action and the spice of life take center stage! We'll blend in like street performers at Mardi Gras. With a touch of genie magic—and to provide an all-around authentic experience—we'll understand the historic language effortlessly!"

"Really?" asked Nilay, impressed.

"Indeed! I do have a knack for doing things right!" said Jai.

"Oh, of course!" agreed Nilay as one eyebrow lifted slightly.

"Believe me. You won't be disappointed. We'll witness the boundless activity of the citizens of Saurashtra!"

Chapter 3

The Trek into Town

Walking along the dirt path, Nilay and Jai were absorbed in chatter. The sun shone at midday. The vibrant green vegetation around them and the clear blue sky made their journey toward town a pleasant one.

The village road they traveled along was well-worn. Animal hoof prints lay imprinted along the entire length of the dirt road. The area's dry climate preserved the various animal tracks. Adjacent to the footprints were straight lines impressed by wooden wheels.

"Town sure is far," said Nilay.

"Yep. The trek is a long one," replied Jai.

The pounding of oxen hooves in the distance sounded and gradually became louder.

"Oh, look!" said Jai. "It's a bullock cart!"

"A what?"

"A wooden cart with wooden wheels pulled by an ox. The driver is going our way. We can hitch a ride!" said Jai.

Nilay turned around to get a look at this ancient Indian form of transport. He and Jai edged toward the side of the road as the bullock cart loaded with melons passed by lazily.

"Come on!" said Jai as he hopped onto the rear of the cart.

"Yikes!" Nilay grabbed the back of the cart and pulled himself upward. He and Jai crouched at opposite ends on the back of the load. The driver steering the cart seemed to have no clue that he had picked up extra cargo. The ox, though, gave a slight groan at the added weight.

The ox leading the bullock cart ambled along, as slow as pleasant-day clouds drift, as the driver steadily made his way toward town. Nilay and Jai conversed animatedly the whole ride. Nilay, immersed in good company, smiled, enjoying the exhilarating freedom of the wide-open spaces.

Nilay peeked around the side of the bullock cart. Just ahead, the edge of town became increasingly visible. He remained fully focused on the lively sights growing larger before him. The boy's knees started bouncing up and down, as he did not know quite what to expect from ancient Indian townsfolk.

The streets narrowed. Wooden houses became visible. People in colorful garments walked and talked everywhere. Cows, goats and monkeys shared the streets with the human town dwellers. Nilay and Jai took gigantic leaps off the wobbly cart.

"This is amazing!" said Nilay in awe. Stalls of all kinds lined the streets. Craftsmen hammered silver into miniature statues and ornaments. Ceramists spun pottery wheels, fashioning ceramic bowls of all shapes and sizes before Nilay's eyes. The bustle of activity occurred out in the open, with artisans working while sitting on rugs on the town's walkways.

A crowd gathered in a circle a few yards ahead. The pounding of drums filled the air. "What's all the commotion?" asked Nilay.

"We shall find out!" replied Jai.

Nilay and Jai hurried toward the gathering. Two muscular men, their skin gleaming with sesame oil, hunched in the center of the ring of people. One of the men swung at his opponent, then flipped him flat onto the ground.

"They're wrestling!" said Nilay with the passion of a sports fan in the stands. Nilay and Jai cheered along with the crowd.

Within ten minutes, one wrestler flung his adversary onto the branch of a nearby tree. The match was over. The standing contender won.

"This is the best wrestling match ever!" said Nilay, beaming.

"Nothing beats watching live wrestling in the year 300 CE!" said Jai. Satisfied with catching ancient sportsmanship in action, Nilay continued walking.

From the corner of Nilay's eye, silvery, writhing ropes alongside the road caught his attention. A small gathering of local children, men and women gathered in the busy market. Nilay approached to get a better look.

On top of a rug sat a bare-chested man with a thick, grayish beard. His long, matted hair was partially twisted in a bun at the top of his head. A single strand of a crudely made seashell necklace hung around the street performer's neck.

Three midsized baskets slightly shifted left and right in front of the man seated cross-legged. He clasped his fingers around a flute made from gourd fruit. The flute spanned two feet, with a large bulb in the center. The street performer brought the flute to his lips and started to play a hypnotizing tune.

"What's he up to?" whispered Nilay to his genie friend. He had never seen the likes of this.

"You're in for a surprise!" Jai snickered.

Just then, from the baskets, the silvery ropes grew taller in stature. The crowd gasped.

"They're snakes!" said Nilay.

"They're not just any snakes. They are king cobras! Watch as the snake charmer entrances the deadliest of snakes!" said Jai.

Playing the flute, the snake charmer swayed to the left, then the right, and continued his melodic enchantment. The three cobras followed the street performer's every graceful move. The audience clapped.

"But snakes don't have ears!" said Nilay, still in disbelief. He had paid attention to his science lessons.

"These reptiles can sense the sound vibrations," replied Jai.

"Look, the cobras are extending their hoods! Won't they bite?"

"In ancient India, snake charmers removed the cobras' fangs or venom. The snakes are harmless. But the audience doesn't know that," said Jai.

Just then, the snake charmer put down his flute. A half coconut shell filled with milk lay next to the snake charmer. The aged street performer gently held the head of one cobra and guided it toward the milk. The snake gulped the milk.

"He's feeding the cobra!" said Nilay. The crowd relished the spectacle. Men and women threw silver and gold coins at the feet of the street performer.

Not too far off, as the crowd dispersed, a new sound captured the wanderers' attention.

"Listen: the clickety-clack of the silk weavers' looms!" squealed Jai.

Chapter 4

The Weaving Looms

THE BUSY CLICK-CLICKS of wooden weaving looms sounded. Seated outside on stools, men and women pushed and pulled the hand looms that towered five feet in height and six feet across.

"See, Nilay! We've stumbled upon the Saurashtrian silk weavers!" said Jai, his voice expressing exuberance.

With wonder, Nilay said, "So this is how silk sarees are made!" A familiar, pleasant feeling enveloped him. His mom wore sarees on special occasions back in Canada, and now he had a chance to learn firsthand how the likes of his mom's fancy apparel were originally fashioned.

"Watch carefully," said Jai, "as they turn silk threads into the most beautiful silk sarees, spanning six yards in length!" Nilay was so entranced, he forgot to take a seat to watch the marvels. Captivated, Nilay stood with Jai, watching the sea of Saurashtrian silk weavers work their magnificent saree art.

"Do you see those women just a few feet from us," said Jai, "wearing plain cotton sarees and standing over enormous buckets filled with colored water?"

Nilay nodded, remaining transfixed by the scene.

"They are the dye masters! These skilled women produce deep blue dyes from the roots of vegetable plants. Over yonder, women fashion ruby-red dyes from shellac, a sort of resin. Those three women soak the silk in buckets of dyes made from turmeric, turning them into sunny yellow threads. See there, those laughing ladies sitting along the edges of the pathways squeeze out emerald-green dyes made from pomegranate rinds. That young woman mixes iron shavings with vinegar and creates dazzling black dyes to make jet black threads."

"This is the traditional way of coloring the threads, a practice that is still used in some parts of modern-day India," said Jai.

Men placed the vibrant, silken threads into the hand looms, interlacing them and working their talents to produce silk sarees. The tireless artisans used pure raw silk, a feature of the best in Saurashtrian silk weaving.

"You know, Nilay, legend has it that the Saurashtrian silk weavers are descendants of the gods' chief weaver, Sage Markanda, who produced fine silks from fibers of the lotus flower," whispered Jai.

Nilay was too engrossed in the scene before him to reply. The newness of the ancient town and watching historic silk weavers in action was like landing on the moon for the young boy.

Jai put his hands on his hips and said, "This is the local craft of the Saurashtrians! As you can see, the industrious

Saurashtrians in ancient India toil honestly and are as happy as the populace of any blissful kingdom can be."

Jai snapped his fingers before Nilay's eyes. Nilay blinked and jumped back, slightly startled. "This scene is just amazing! Sorry, I was absorbed in the saree making. I've never seen the likes of it before!" said Nilay.

"Of course, you haven't! We've traveled, oh, only about seventeen hundred years back in time. And," said Jai, "you've never been outside of your Canadian province!"

"Well, I'm glad I'm here," said Nilay with a sheepish smile.

"You know, Nilay," said Jai, "among the Saurashtrians is a peaceful community of the best silk weavers and silk merchants in India. Most of the community are involved in the silk trade. This community of Saurashtrian artisans is so skilled at its craft that weaving comes as naturally as breathing to young and old alike. In fact, to Saurashtrians of the day, silk weaving is an inborn gift, passed down from generation to generation."

"Look!" said Nilay, pointing to an iridescent peacock-colored saree bordered in gold. The cloth featured a design boasting a metallic geometric pattern. "How the material shimmers!"

"That's real gold thread woven into the saree," said Jai. Gold and silver threads dazzled whenever the light shone upon the silken cloth.

"Watch this," said Jai. He dug deep into his pockets and produced a yellowish powder. The newbie genie flung the powder onto the peacock design sewn into a saree laying to the side. As soon as the powder hit the silk, a dazzling bluish-green peacock stepped out from the silken cloth.

"Jai! That's amazing!" said Nilay, delighted, as if he were a guest at a live magic show. "What a treat!"

"Oh, it's only a little genie trick that I learned from Dad," said Jai. The genie bowed his head and said, "Now I know that I can do it, too! It's kind of a special moment."

"Aww," said Nilay, recognizing how dads influence their proud little boys. He thought of how much his dad adored him. A feeling of wholeness and love filled Nilay.

Jai lightly jabbed Nilay, distracting him from his reflections. "You know, Nilay, the peacock is the royal emblem of the Maurya Empire."

"You're always ready with a fun story, Jai! And, as you can tell, I'm always ready to listen," replied Nilay, picking up a peacock feather that had dropped to the ground. The boy playfully stuck the plume behind his ear. Nilay glanced over at his genie companion for approval of his choice of embellishment for his short, black locks.

"Genie-in-training approved!" laughed Jai.

With an audience, the bird paraded about for a bit, then found a shady spot and unfolded its regal plumage, its mesmerizing eyespots marking the tips of each feather. Wanting to capture this precious moment with this prized bird in its homeland, Nilay brought out his phone for a quick photo. The bird stopped in its tracks and posed for a rare glamour shot.

"You know, Nilay, in India, the peacock is a familiar symbol of grace, love and beauty. It's no wonder you are so charmed by it!" said Jai.

The stunning display was a sight to behold. Nilay gasped again in awe, as this was his first ever live sighting of the magnificent peacock. The bird cocked its head to the side and strutted off. Nilay turned, watching the magic of his genie friend disappear into the bushes.

Intrigued by its natural splendor, Nilay followed the bird.

To Nilay, the bird seemed to embody all that was good. He had to get closer to this wild creature.

Jai screamed after Nilay, "Hey! Where are you going?"

Chapter 5

The Peacock Encounter

"I WANT TO GET a video, too!" yelled Nilay. The bird's gait increased as Nilay intently darted after it with his phone in hand. Without warning, the peacock stopped in its tracks, turned, unfolded its mighty feathers and glared at Nilay. With its feathers fully spread, it was a superb sight to behold; but the bird's piercing glower, along with its sharp beak, was nothing short of intimidating.

The bird's image became visible on Nilay's phone screen.

He naively flipped the phone so the screen faced the creature.

Nilay said, "See, lovely bird! It's you!"

Jogging close behind Nilay was Jai. The genie, panting, yelled out a warning. "Peacocks can get fierce, Ni—!"

Before Jai could finish his sentence, the peacock lunged

toward Nilay, pecking at his phone.

A startled Nilay gripped his phone tightly and flung his arm into the air to evade damage to the device. He scrambled away hurriedly, climbing on top of a low tree branch. His heart pounded rapidly.

At this point, Jai caught up. Still out of breath, he said, "The peacock saw its image on your phone. Not being the cleverest of birds, the peacock figured it was another peacock, so it attacked!"

The peacock flew away once the supposed competition disappeared. Nilay slowly inched off the tree branch that protected him and his device from harm.

"You're lucky the peacock barely missed scratching you," said Jai. "In 300 CE India, well-equipped hospitals are nonexistent!"

Nilay breathed a sigh of relief. He put his phone back into his pocket. Easy to please and understanding that animals have their ways, too, Nilay smiled and said, "It was worth it. What a story to tell! An ancient Indian peacock gave me a run for it!"

Jai clapped his hands and threw up his arms. "Okay, back to wish making...wish granting....The terms are just as diverse as the wishes themselves," said the newbie genie. Invigorated by the peacock run-in that he'd never experience at home in Toronto, Nilay returned with Jai to the spot where the throng of artisans busily worked.

"Now, there are no such things as unhappy customers when they buy from the silk weavers of Saurashtra," said Jai with a grin.

"I bet the silk sarees don't come with peacocks that magically make an entrance!" quipped Nilay. He then shifted his attention to the sarees being woven before his eyes. "I know my mom would love a silk saree," said the boy, wistfully.

Thinking of his parents, a boost of confidence overcame him. He continued, "Mom said that on their wedding day, Dad dressed like an Indian prince. And Dad said Mom looked like an Indian princess!"

"Ah! True love," sighed Jai. The novice genie pointed one finger up and said, "Speaking of princes, the Saurashtrian artisans also weave the most handsome traditional menswear!"

"Like what?" asked Nilay.

"Like silk salwar kameez, you know, men's clothing that's similar to long tunics and matching pants."

"Ah, yes, I can picture that," said Nilay.

Jai continued, "They weave pure white silk dhotis trimmed with gold."

"Dhotis?" asked Nilay.

"You'll find dhotis worn in India. Dhotis are like kilts or pleated pants. Men have worn them since ancient times. You're pretty Canadianized, aren't you?" said Jai.

"I sure am. But I love learning about history," said Nilay. Without missing a beat, he asked, "Did kings wear silk dhotis?"

"In the earliest Indian empires, they certainly did!" replied Jai. "Also, stately silk headdresses, like turbans, are made to wrap around a man's head."

"Turbans? My dad doesn't wear turbans," said Nilay.

"In ancient India, silk turbans are ornamental embellishments that reveal a man's level of prestige," said Jai. "How the turban is wrapped indicates his rank among the townspeople."

"People wear turbans of different colors, too, to show their status?" asked Nilay.

"Correct! Turbans also serve a practical purpose—they keep the heat of India's blazing sun off the men's heads," said Jai.

"Ah, right. That makes sense. It *is* really hot here!" said Nilay. "You don't suppose there's a vending machine nearby where I can get a bottle of water?"

Jai smacked his hand upon his head. "Nilay, my friend and master, the only thing closest to a vending machine in 300 CE India is…" Jai scanned the landscape and spotted a water source a few yards away. "That drinking well!" Casually, they both walked toward it, chatting the whole time.

"You know, although the Saurashtrians were mostly silk weavers and silk merchants, a small number of them were Brahmin priests," said Jai.

"Holy men? Holy moly!" said Nilay, impressed by the range of noble pursuits for which the Saurashtrians were known.

"Yep. Their rich knowledge of the religious poems, like the Vedas, written thousands of years ago, won them the esteem of the kings and their courts."

They stopped at the terraced steps of the stepwell. Nilay cupped his hands and dipped them into the water. He quenched his thirst with ancient India's well water.

"You know, I've got a trick up my sleeve!" said Jai.

As Nilay sat on the steps of the well, sudden goosebumps covered his arms.

Chapter 6

The Dip in the Drinking Well

THE DIM SHADE OF evening gradually closed upon the day. Under the light of the full moon, Nilay's reflection shone on the still waters of the well.

Large, manmade stepwells dotted the landscape in these parts of western India. Visitors to the wells could reach the water by descending flights of steps up to thirteen stories deep built along the four sides of the square ponds.

Many stepwells were famed for being architecturally spectacular. Perfectly geometric in design, some stepwells featured intricate carvings along every level. Even the plainest of stone steps awed visitors. When the heavy rains neglected to fill the wells, the stepwells' beauty could be appreciated far more.

In the stepwell from which Nilay drank, the rainwaters had filled the basin to its brim, making it easy to get a refreshing drink from the uppermost level. The surface of the well water appeared serene against the agitated, darkened sky.

"Master and friend, I've never tried this before, this being my very first wish…" said Jai.

"I'm listening," said Nilay patiently.

"Well, I'm about to show you a scene, a moment of masterful triumph and equally great defeat," said Jai.

"Hmmm," said Nilay, as he scratched his head, not sure what to expect from his genie friend.

"First, let me paint the picture," said Jai. "For hundreds of years after this very moment in history, the Saurashtrians lived peacefully and prospered."

Nilay started to yawn.

"Then," continued Jai, like a master storyteller, "in this very region, the year 1027 CE put a peg in the smoothly turning wheel."

"What happened?" asked Nilay, as he perked up with the news of some formidable force.

Matter-of-factly, Jai said, "Mahmud Ghazni happened."

"Who's Mahmud Ghazni?" asked Nilay.

"Mahmud Ghazni was a Turkish conqueror. He invaded India seventeen times! With each raid, he plundered various regions of their gold, silver and gems. His empire grew wealthier and mightier with every invasion."

"He traveled all the way from Turkey on foot?" asked Nilay.

"Oh no, my master and friend! Ghazni's men rode swift horses. The conqueror's cavalry overtook their Indian enemies with speed and precision."

Billowy clouds moved fast across the night sky, disguising the moon, so that moments of complete darkness prevailed. When the moonlight shone, Jai continued his story with wide eyes and a hushed tone.

"During Ghazni's very last, and, I might add, biggest invasion of India, he overtook Saurashtra," said Jai.

Nilay gave a quick gasp, surprised that such a peaceful region could withstand a savage enemy king.

"The warrior king plundered a major temple, called Somnath, along the Saurashtrian coastline. He looted every nook and cranny of the temple, viciously battled the Indian army and seized their wealth," said Jai.

Just then, the full moon reflected perfectly in the waters of the drinking well near the steps where Nilay and Jai sat. Not a single haze blocked the pale sphere in the darkened sky. The hairs on Nilay's arms stood up. He sensed he was on the verge of a thrill.

"By the light of the full moon, you will witness the pillage, the horses and the barbarism of Mahmud Ghazni," said Jai.

Nilay shook with anticipation. A slight fear overcame him for just a second.

Jai continued, "This is where my trick comes in!"

The tension left Nilay's body, and he let out a loud exhale. "Oh, it's just a trick. That's a relief!" he said.

"I hope it goes right. We shall see!" Jai whisked a magic hat and wand out of thin air. He put the hat on his head and held the wand in his hand. "These are just for effect!" said Jai with a wink, as he motioned his hands around the waters.

Nilay chuckled. Jai tipped his magic hat at his friend.

The sound of galloping horses' stomping feet suddenly vanquished the night's silence. A battalion of ferocious Turkish troops on horseback wielded swords as they rode across the land. Indian soldiers mounted on armored elephants slowly fought back.

Nilay witnessed this warfare on the surface of the water. These scenes took place in front of Nilay's eyes, as if the top of the well was another world. The moonlit water was a canvas. The moon reflected in perfect position on the water, as if it were shining at the scene of the battle itself.

"We're safe from a distance," said Jai. "I might have to say I'm quite good! Being a genie is a cinch!" The apprentice genie sat back, folded his arms across his chest, closed his eyes and relaxed.

Like any young schoolboy, Nilay was fascinated, not only with his genie friend's magic but at the sight of the battle. He dared not even blink for fear he'd miss an extraordinary scene. All these moments were nothing short of astounding!

Nilay steadily watched the ancient invasion take place right before his eyes. Ghazni's swift horses were no match for the Indian army's slow-moving elephants.

Nilay was absorbed in the clash. The moonlit waters showed the scene of an Indian soldier falling from his charging elephant. The soldier let out a yell as a Turkish cavalryman approached with a sword in hand, ready to plunge it into the heart of his enemy.

The kindhearted Nilay jumped at the sight of the fighter's defenselessness. Nilay stretched out his hand toward the fallen Indian soldier to help him up. Just then, Jai opened his eyes.

"No!" Jai burst out.

But it was too late. Nilay had reached too far. Plunging into the one-hundred-foot well, Nilay screamed for Jai. "Help! Jai! I can't swim!"

Jai jumped to his feet and scrambled toward the edge of the well. Nilay failed to tread water. He was sinking fast. Reacting quickly, Jai did the only thing he could do to save his friend and master. He held out his hand.

In the nick of time, Nilay grabbed Jai's outstretched hand. Instantly, they both vanished.

Chapter 7
The Ghazni Invasion

THUD!

Nilay and Jai fell onto a sandy dune. Dawn was just breaking.

"Uh-oh," said Jai.

"Oh no, now where are we?" asked Nilay, as he got up and brushed off the dust from his cargo pants.

"It's more about *when* than where we are," said Jai. "We're...in...the year...1027 CE!"

A stampede of horses ran past, ridden by men wielding long swords. "And..." said Jai with a shudder, "we're in the midst of the Ghazni invasion!"

"What?" said Nilay.

"Run!" screamed Jai.

War elephants with swords attached to their trunks were

forced ahead by Indian soldiers. Ghazni horses reared back in fright at the line of huge elephants that formed an impenetrable barricade.

Nilay and Jai scrambled across the battlefield, too short to be taken seriously by either Indian or Turkish warriors. But they were far from safe. A single step of an elephant storming the front lines could squash Nilay or Jai in a second.

A fire arrow shot by an Indian archer whizzed past Jai's ear. "This isn't sounding too good!" said a trembling Jai.

The Indian army consisted of not only war elephants, but mounted cavalry. Elite Indian warriors on horseback were so skilled, they shot from steel bows. With the speed of light, these bows pierced the thickest Turkish armor. Commoner warriors shot with expert ability using bamboo longbows.

Ghazni's forces fought on horseback. The ferocious Turkish warriors used tactile defense strategies to weaken the Indian fighters.

Stuck in the middle of the battlefield, Jai ran left, then right. His little genie head spun in confusion. A Turkish cavalryman with a furrowed brow and lance in hand charged at Jai, as if to practice using his weaponry on a moving but sure target.

The thundering rumble of elephants' feet grew louder and louder. Warriors shrieked battle calls. Out of the blue, Nilay screamed his own battle cry, "No you don't!" From atop a charging elephant, Nilay reached down, grabbed Jai's vest and plucked the genie from the battleground. The enemy on horseback sped past.

"Mm—mas—master!" said Jai, shaken but relieved. Nilay had managed to climb upon the back of a war elephant, sharing the beast with four well-built Indian archers.

Now, both Nilay and Jai found a brief spell of safety on

the back of the massive animal. The archers were too consumed with defending themselves and fighting for their land to notice the two little extra passengers.

"There! A tree! Quick, jump when we pass!" yelled Nilay. The elephant lunged forward.

As soon as the giant animal passed under the tree, Nilay and Jai jumped. Their arms caught the thick branch of the tree. Holding on, they both pulled themselves up and sat high in the safety of the tree.

Nilay and Jai had a clear view of the battle zone.

The warriors of India held large shields carved with fiery dragons. The enormous shields, as large as the combatants themselves, protected the unarmored Indian soldiers from the Turkish invaders' swords.

Turkish horses scattered at the fearsome sight of the great Indian elephants, but the soldiers regrouped. Ghazni's swift cavalrymen surrounded the Indian warriors. After hours of bloodshed, the brave Indian troops were defeated.

Ghazni's warriors fearlessly strode into the Somnath temple compound. They looted the temple of its vast riches and retreated, far wealthier than they had become on any of their previous conquests.

The sun tranquilly raised its glorious head. After the deadly whir of dawn, the morning's calm embraced the land.

"We can't hang around here," said Nilay, still sitting in the tree. He looked out into the horizon. A small group of Saurashtrians was traveling south. The gifted silk weavers, honest silk merchants and respected Brahmin priests had gathered their precious silks, weaving looms and sacred texts, piled them onto bullock carts and began the trek to India's southern region of Maharashtra.

Following Nilay's gaze, Jai spotted the caravan of people

and said, "They are fleeing to avoid more bloodshed from the tyrant Ghazni."

And so, the Saurashtrians' most significant migration began.

Jai, with an apologetic tone in his voice, said, "My friend and master, plopping down in the epicenter of peril was hardly in the original plan! Being frazzled by the sudden chaos, the thought of disappearing as soon as we landed fled my mind."

"No worries," replied Nilay. "In a way, it was like playing soldier—but with far more excitement. What other kid in my hometown can say he was on the inside of a historic military battle!"

Jai continued, "Your outlook does you wonders, Nilay. We'll get your saree with the help of the Saurashtrian silk weavers!"

With the fervor of a pirate captain on the brink of rediscovering a lost treasure, Nilay quivered with anticipation, instinctively knowing their quest for the perfect red silk saree had just begun.

Chapter 8

The Chess Game

"WELL," SAID NILAY, NOW accustomed to surprises—intended or not—from his novice genie friend. He leaned back to rest against the trunk of the massive banyan tree. "What happened to the Saurashtrians that migrated into present-day Maharashtra?"

The tender leaves flourishing on the banyan tree provided cool shade for the duo under the sweltering Indian sun.

Jai, looking for a comfortable seat, shifted and prepared to tell the vibrant story of the Saurashtrian silk weavers.

"Little did the Saurashtrians know that this was Ghazni's last invasion of India. Still, because of the unrest spurred by this Ghazni raid, many peace-loving Saurashtrians decided to leave the region," said Jai.

"He did invade India seventeen times. Why would anyone

want to stay behind with the likes of Ghazni lurking around?" asked Nilay.

Jai said, "Right. The Saurashtrian silk weavers lived with peace and prosperity for hundreds of years before the Ghazni invasion. Though love of their land gave them reason to stay, the peaceful community felt a stronger urge to shift five hundred miles southward to a protected fort city in India's Maharashtra."

A few monkeys scampered about on the ground, looking for a bite to eat. Nilay stuck his hands into his pockets. The dates he had gathered not too long ago were still there. He grabbed a few and tossed them to the hungry monkeys. The skinny animals scurried to take away the sweet fruit.

Nilay relaxed on the branch of the banyan tree, staring into the cloudless, grand sky above. Jai also dug his hands into his pockets. He pulled out a nail clipper, a cake pan, a handheld radio, a chess board with chess pieces and a hockey stick.

"Don't need any of these," said Jai, shrugging and tossing the miscellaneous rubbish one by one out onto the barren landscape. The inquisitive monkeys darted toward the medley of junk.

Nilay eyed the chess board laying among scattered pawns, bishops, rooks, kings and knights. He thought for a moment and said, "You know, Jai, I've never played chess with a genie, let alone an apprentice genie. How about a match?"

"Oh, oh! You want to battle the wits of a novice genie, eh?" snarked Jai. "Bring it on, good chap!"

The two leaped off the banyan tree and gathered the strewn chess pieces and the checkered board. Setting up the board on a large, flat rock, Nilay and Jai hunched over and strategized intensely, like master chess players.

Nilay, having invited Jai to the chess match, said, "Your

move first, Jai." The genie-in-training moved his knight, an unusual initial tactic.

"This promises to be a challenge!" said Nilay as he advantageously positioned his pawn. The game continued under the unhurriedly moving clouds. The atmosphere was peaceful. The only energy in the desert-like environment arose from the duo intensely focused on playing the ancient game of chess.

Jai brought out his rook, a decisive move, making Nilay's queen vulnerable to attack. Nilay responded by horizontally moving his own rook and capturing one of Jai's knights.

The game continued. Only a few pieces—a knight, the kings and a few pawns—remained on the board, with Nilay having captured many of Jai's pieces. Jai rubbed his palms together, as if to bring good luck, stared intently at the enemy king and moved his knight forward. The second Jai touched the knight, a low rumble broke the stillness.

In unison, the two said, "What was that?"

The knight piece on the board started to shake. Nilay stared at the commotion on the chess board. "Jai," he said slowly and guardedly, still staring at the shaking knight piece, "what did you do?"

Before Jai could respond, a stream of smoke shot out of the center of the knight piece and bolted into the sky. Out of the smoke emerged a horse mounted by a knight in full armor, holding a sharpened lance. The horse, straddled by its knight, fell to the ground and galloped speedily toward the chess players, the knight's lance aimed directly toward Nilay and Jai.

Jai's eyes nearly popped out of his head at the sight. "I...I...don't know...what I did," said the newbie genie, trembling.

"He's coming straight at us! To the knight, we must be

expendable. Jai, you don't know your own powers!" screamed Nilay. "Quick, rub your hands again and touch the king," said Nilay. The boy was almost in a panic.

The novice genie did as he was instructed. A blast of smoke streamed out of the king piece. A stately man of huge proportions, wearing a thick cloak and a crown, appeared. The king moved sparingly.

The knight in armor shifted his focus to the king, aiming to defeat him and win. Nilay's words escaped hastily. "Jai, do the same for the two pawns!"

Two foot soldiers appeared with the same ferocity as the knight and king. These two pawns stood in front of the king, resolved to defend.

Nilay and Jai watched as the offensive knight headed straight for the king. The foot soldiers wielded their weapons, ready as defensive pieces.

Looking at the chess board and thinking quickly, Nilay said to Jai, "Hurry, we must finish the game before the knight vanquishes the king and turns his attention toward us!"

With rapid fire, Nilay and Jai took turns moving their chess pieces. Nilay's pawn captured Jai's knight. In the blitz, the knight that appeared on horseback disappeared with a poof.

"We're at endgame!" exclaimed Nilay. He moved his pawn next to Jai's king. "Check!" said Nilay. Jai's king immediately captured Nilay's pawn. One foot soldier disappeared. The game was yet unfinished. Finally, Nilay was in the position to yell, "Checkmate!" With Jai's king wiped out, Nilay won the game. Instantly, the king and remaining foot soldier vanished without a trace.

Nilay breathed a sigh of relief. He smiled and looked at his genie comrade, who also let out a loud exhalation and said, "Oh, the things an apprentice genie learns through experience."

For a few moments, the two sat in disbelief. "Well, you know, it was a teachable moment," said Nilay.

Jai said, "That's for sure!"

Casually, Jai put his hands into his pockets again. This time, his fingers felt the coolness of a glass dome. "What's this?" he asked. Jai pulled the glass ball out.

"It looks like a crystal ball!" said Nilay.

"Hmmm," said Jai, scratching his chin. He turned the glass ball around, examining every inch. "Indeed, it might be!"

They both peered into the glass ball.

Inside, the crystal ball flashed vivid scenes of Indian people clad in cotton and of battles that took place in the great land of the Saurashtrian silk weavers. "This is India's future from this moment on," whispered Jai, focusing intensely on the activity inside the ball.

"This crystal ball is revealing the next three hundred years!" said Jai. "See there, the mysterious Hun invaders are taking over. And there, the magnificent Gupta dynasty loses power!"

"India sure went through a lot of rulers," said Nilay.

"And look, there! The ball is showing Marco Polo, the Venetian merchant, arriving on India's southwestern coast! He is praising Gujarat's merchants as the most honest in the world," said Jai, his eyes wide with excitement. Apparently, Jai hadn't known he possessed a magical crystal ball hiding in his pockets.

Nilay spent the afternoon captivated by the scenes of Indian history taking place with vivid realism right before his eyes, in the center of the trainee genie's recently discovered crystal ball.

Then he saw a new empire, ruled by multiple secessions of dynasties, take hold in the south.

"What was royal life like in India?" asked Nilay. Both Nilay and Jai still sat upon the sun-warmed ground at the base of the tree.

"Well, since my first trick failed to pan out just right, I've got another trick up my sleeve to answer your question!" said Jai, sheepishly smiling.

"First off, Jai, your sleeves look too short to hold a bag of tricks." Nilay laughed.

"True." Jai chuckled, looking at his vest.

"And second," said Nilay, "you could brush up on your tricks!"

"You know, we could keep walking."

"To where?" asked Nilay.

"To experience royal life in ancient India firsthand," said Jai.

"You mean follow the Saurashtrians to the south?"

"Or we could just fly," said Jai as he scuttled a few feet away, turning his back to Nilay.

Nilay's expression was mixed with wonder and exhilaration at the thought of flying. He didn't have to consider the promise of a sky-bound adventure for long. Nilay rushed toward his genie friend. He tapped Jai on the shoulder. Jai quickly turned around.

His face beaming with joy, Nilay said, "I'm ready. Let's fly!"

With full trust in his fresh-faced genie friend and his equally unripe abilities, Nilay held out his hand. Jai grasped it. Both vanished from the arid environment.

The onlooking monkeys stopped in their tracks. The bewildered primates scampered around the spot where the two friends disappeared and scratched their itty-bitty heads.

Chapter 9
The Flight

"OOMPH!" UTTERED NILAY. "NOT a bad landing this time around!"

Jai's piloting skills had significantly improved. He and Nilay fell with a slight thump onto a soft, cushioned surface. The material was that of a velvety blue carpet trimmed in decorative silver—a floating carpet.

"Now this is exactly the kind of hocus-pocus that makes a genie's day!" said Jai, his head held high. His latest trick had succeeded. Nilay and Jai kneeled in the middle of a flying carpet, soaring above a vast kingdom. Royal inhabitants, splendidly dressed in colorful clothes and gold ornaments, walked about the royal city, appearing as tiny as miniature dolls.

As they soared through the clouds, Jai offered a nugget of history. "Even before the brilliant dawn of the first millennium,

India had been a sophisticated, advanced land. The colorful country boasted countless kingdoms, both vast and small, spotted with lavish palaces. We have landed here, along the southwestern part of India, in a region speckled with innumerable forts. It is the year 1336 CE," said Jai.

"Whoohoo!" yelled Nilay. He and Jai sailed clear across the blue sky. "You're a genius genie!" screamed Nilay, laughing and throwing his arms gleefully into the air as he ascended into the cloudless skies.

The duo flew toward a greenish haze moving gently in midair. Upon flying closer, Nilay discovered they were speeding past a flock of cotton pygmy geese. The birds squawked. Nilay turned and grinned at the fowl left trailing behind. In prompt response, the geese trumpeted in disharmonious accord.

"What great part of India are we in now?" asked Nilay, relishing the freedom of flight and the rush of wind against his rosy cheeks.

"We are hovering over…over…" Jai pulled a map out of thin air. He studied it for a minute, pointed to a spot at the middle of the map, then shifted his fingers toward the bottom and replied, "Gracious golly! We are flying over the imposing Vijayanagara Empire!"

"Awesome! Tell me you can steer this flying carpet, Jai!" said Nilay, whizzing along the sweeping atmosphere.

"Oh, um…that wasn't part of the original plan," said Jai, his worried voice trailing. It appeared that the concept of navigating the carpet had just dawned on the genie. "This being my first carpet ride, I hadn't really thought quite that far!"

Alarmed, Nilay screamed, "What!"

The flying carpet seemed to have a mind of its own. Jai grabbed hold of the tassels at the carpet's front corners and attempted to steer. "This isn't working!" said Jai as he pulled at the tassels to steer toward the left and then the right with all his might. "The carpet's a dud!"

They zoomed past hilltop fortresses and watchtowers. The guards inside did double takes when the duo whizzed past with the speed of light. Scarcely believing what they saw, the sentinels mistook Nilay and Jai for exotic birds clutching nesting material in their talons.

Nilay's eyes popped. His fear grew over the possibility that they would smash into the palace walls, a tree or one of the city's one hundred and forty sacred sites.

Before either Nilay or Jai could blink, the carpet zoomed over multiple stone fortifications, commoners selling their wares in countless bazaars, pilgrims on trips and imperial officers briskly walking about and discussing important matters in efforts to administer the kingdom.

"Uh-oh!" said Nilay. The flying carpet sped downward,

inching closer to the kingdom's urban core.

Within moments, Nilay and Jai approached a magnificent palace built several stories high. They barely missed colliding with the palace's eighty-foot pillars.

Nilay looked back and heaved a sigh of relief. "Phew!"

But before he could turn around again, *SMACK!* The front of the carpet smashed low into a wall in the palace courtyard. Nilay and Jai lunged forward. The carpet instantly crinkled in the collision and heaved the friends off its surface. The two fell a mere foot onto the ground. The flying carpet spun quickly and then collapsed.

Nilay and Jai, though slightly dazed, were unhurt. Jai recovered his wits. Nilay's cheeks flushed beet red.

In a clear attempt to appease the flustered Nilay, Jai smiled wide, threw up his hands and said, "Uh, welcome to the Vijayanagara Empire!"

His brows furrowed and his lips pursed, Nilay threw a glance at Jai. By now, Nilay had started to get used to Jai's minor inconsistencies when it came to performing novice genie tricks. Jai was a newbie genie, after all, and this was what Nilay had signed up for. A carpet crash, though, did not sit too well with him. He dared not entertain the thought of possibly having to return to Canada with a broken nose or thumb. Still, he was ready to bounce back after each disaster, no matter how trivial or huge.

"Come! Let us explore," said Jai as he put on a tan hat and khaki shirt—the gear of a wildlife safari tour guide.

"Well, if you put it that way," said Nilay, quickly forgiving the near disaster. The frustration of crashing into the palace walls was long behind him.

Ready for another round of uncommon experiences, Nilay shouted, "I'm all in for exploration!"

Chapter 10

The Royal Invitation

CHILDREN'S VOICES BOUNCED OFF the walls around the corner in the courtyard. A small glass marble rolled toward Nilay's feet. He picked it up, looked at it and shot it back toward the sound of laughing children.

"They're shooting marbles!" squealed Nilay as he peered around the pillar. Royal children took refuge in the shady corners of the sun-drenched courtyards, engaged in competitive play.

The sightseeing duo strolled along during the mid-morning hours, beholding the spectacular sights of the majestic palace into which they were haphazardly thrown.

Princes clad in silky whites practiced the regal sport of archery, taking aim at bullseyes in the open-air courts.

In a far room in the palace, three devout princesses sat on

thick cushions, studying philosophy and religion.

A fourth princess, dripping with jewels, sought counsel with an advisor, as she served as a provincial ruler under the king. "My mom would be an out-of-this-world ruler, if she were in this time and place," said Nilay proudly.

"I bet she would!" replied Jai with a giggle. Their trip so far had proved to be enlightening.

Nilay and Jai soon stumbled upon the palace's queen. Giving orders left and right, she busily tended to daily life at court, ensuring the royal cooks prepared sumptuous, hearty vegetarian meals.

"You know what I notice?" asked Nilay, nudging his genie friend with his elbow.

"What could you possibly notice in an unfamiliar land that's almost seven hundred years back in history?" asked Jai, with a hint of playful sarcasm.

"Well, everyone in the kingdom glitters in the most handsome clothing, from the princes to the queen!"

"That's easy to explain," said Jai, with the air of a history professor. "This is due, in large part, to the Saurashtrian silk weavers and silk merchants."

"Oh, that's right!" exclaimed Nilay, recalling the skirmish moments of his breathtaking adventure. "They had migrated to the southwestern part of India after the Ghazni invasions! And now you're saying they're here, within this kingdom?"

"Indeed, I am," said Jai. "You see, Nilay, in ancient times like these, only the royal families wear silk."

"What do the non-royals wear?"

"Commoners wear cotton, for the most part," said Jai. "Did you like my wordplay with that?" Jai winked.

Nilay groaned.

Jai continued his explanation. "Since the Saurashtrians

consistently wove the most exquisite silks in the region, the Vijayanagara Empire's kings and their families took notice. Eventually, the kings and their palace dwellers became loyal patrons of the Saurashtrians' first-rate artistry. Over time, the Saurashtra community of silk weavers became the treasured royal weavers."

"Royal weavers," repeated Nilay, delighting in the sound and imagery the combination of words produced.

Men's deep voices suddenly broke the carefree tone of Nilay and Jai's conversation. As the friends walked up a short flight of stone steps, they approached the palace's royal throne room.

"Shhh," said Nilay. He and Jai tiptoed toward the edge of the doorway. "It sounds important!"

Inside, the Vijayanagara king spoke with confidence to his trusted court adviser. "We must unify the empire." The king wore a silken stitched garment underneath an elegant silk coat encrusted with rubies, pearls and emeralds. A silk turban graced his head.

The advisor, more plainly dressed, yet still looking impressive, said, "It is possible!"

The king said, "We must shift the capital of the empire. We can no longer administer the empire from here, in Anegundi. Our center of governance is vulnerable to attack from the north. The new capital will be along the protected south banks of the Tungabhadra River—in Vijayanagara."

"We shall have it done, my lord!" said the advisor, tinkering with the scarf lying over his silken tunic.

The king noticed the advisor's silk apparel, looked at his own and said, "And invite the Saurashtrian silk weavers to join us near our palace in the new capital. We value their silks and honesty highly. The palace dwellers will be far too upset without the silks produced by our most accomplished weavers!"

"All will be done, Your Majesty. It is important the royals look like royals!" said the humble advisor. He added, with a burst of confidence, "We shall issue a royal invitation today."

Before the advisor could take his leave, Nilay scrambled down the steps, with Jai following. Walking along the palace halls, Nilay thought out loud, "I wonder…"

"What do you wonder, my friend?" asked Jai.

"What would it be like to be an ancient Indian prince for a day?"

Jai considered it for a moment. Before he could answer, Nilay turned into the vacant room of one of the princes. The prince's silken white clothing lay on the bed.

"Hmmm," said Nilay. "I'll try this on." He put on the silken clothing over his T-shirt and pants. Nilay then carefully wrapped a white turban around his head. "I think it goes something like this," he said, making a solid first attempt to properly wrap the turban.

"Well? Do you feel like a prince?" asked Jai.

"Almost," said Nilay. The boy walked out of the prince's quarters and into the courtyard. The princes had interrupted their archery practice to enjoy lunch. There, in the center of the courtyard, was a large bullseye. A bow and arrow lay on the ground.

Nilay picked up the bow and arrow. "Now I'll know what it feels like to be a true prince!"

The courtyard was right between the royal kitchen and the royal family members' dining hall. A heavy-set palace chef, carrying a silver platter loaded with steaming rice and yogurt, walked across the edges of the courtyard toward the dining area.

Nilay released the bow from the arrow, aiming for the bullseye. The wayward arrow shot past the target. At that moment, the chef dropped the bowl of yogurt. He bent to pick it up. His rear end was far more enormous than the bullseye. The arrow pierced the chef in the backside.

"Bingo!" yelled Jai.

"Uh-oh," said Nilay, with all seriousness.

The chef's face turned as red as the curry Nilay had noticed him serve the royal household just moments before. The chef reached toward his rear end and yanked out the arrow. With the arrow clutched tightly in his fist and his bloodshot eyes bulging, he turned toward Nilay and Jai. Steam escaped from his nostrils.

"Gotta run!" said Nilay. He flung off the turban and the prince's silken clothing. Left in his T-shirt and pants, Nilay made a run for it through the palace halls with Jai following.

The palace corridors were cool in comparison to the scorching courtyard. Here, Nilay ducked into a vacant room. It happened to be a princess's quarters. Inside, dozens of pearl necklaces littered the top of an elaborate dresser, drapes trimmed with golden stitches hung along the windows and a full-length mirror took up a large portion of the room.

The chef followed, running as briskly as his stodgy figure would allow. His face was still beet red, and he wielded the silver platter as if he were ready to clonk it upon Nilay's head if he caught him.

Once inside the princess's room, Nilay dove under a pile of clothing on the floor. Jai, too, accompanied him under it. Nilay peeked out. The chef ran past.

"Phew!" said Nilay.

"Phew is right!" said Jai. "I think the coast is clear."

Sniffing the air inside the princess's quarters, Nilay experienced a sense of calmness. "What is that wonderful scent?"

Jai, too, sampled the air with his nose. "Ah! That aromatic fragrance is the famed sandalwood! The princess must have a habit of smearing her skin with the sweet-smelling sandalwood paste. It's customary for ancient Indians to wear sandalwood as perfume."

Nilay took a look at the clothing that had concealed him from the angry chef. "These are sarees!" said the boy. "They are beautiful!"

"Indeed, they are sarees, and they are undoubtedly lovely! The sarees saved us!" said Jai.

The two friends looked at each other. Nilay instantly recognized the purpose of his journey would, before long, be fulfilled. Jai whispered, "We shall find your perfect red silk saree soon!"

Chapter 11

Life in the Imperial City

LIFE WAS GRAND FOR the kings and their families during peacetime—it was an especially golden time for the Saurashtrians, too.

Nilay and Jai strolled about the magnificent kingdom, meandering past six walled fortifications to reach the outer limits of the imperial city. Taking this route, they witnessed the Saurashtrian silk weavers producing heaps of silk sarees, silk salwar kameez and silk turbans.

"The royal weavers sure are a dedicated bunch," exclaimed Nilay, gazing at the extraordinary output of shimmery silks.

"You know, each morning, the talented Saurashtrian weavers sit at massive outdoor looms, creating gorgeous pieces of silk cloth. Sarees, in a dazzling spectacle of colors and sensational patterns, are woven like clockwork," said Jai, pulling out a ticking clock face that sounded a bell tone when another silk saree was completed.

"It's just like when they were in the Saurashtra region," said Nilay.

"Right on, my friend and master!" replied Jai.

Men dressed in richly dyed silk clothes and striking turbans, their mustaches perfectly groomed to achieve slight twirls at the ends, packed the silken wares into bullock carts.

"Who are those guys?" asked Nilay.

"Saurashtrian silk merchants, Nilay! These fabulous folks work with the Saurashtrian silk weavers. The merchants are highly ethical, and their uprightness is prized by the royal families!"

The two friends stood in awe as oxen effortlessly pulled the lightweight sarees and fine Indian menswear on wooden carts along the dusty roads toward the palace. The merchants headed toward the spot from where Nilay and Jai had just come.

Not intending to miss a piece of history, Nilay scrambled back toward the roads with Jai, catching up with the slow-moving bullock carts.

They inched toward the gates of the palace along with the precious cargo. Standing behind a pillar, Nilay and Jai peeked out. Their close vantage point gave them first-rate views of the inside the palace's lavish interior. In the vast expanse, the duo was just a barely visible speck. Nilay and Jai watched the transaction between the royal family and silk merchants. The event triggered excitement in the air.

For Nilay, seeing important details of untold antiquity unfold before his eyes was like being a captive audience at a highly anticipated epic film.

"Popcorn or chocolate-covered mints? What will you

have?" asked Jai.

"Very funny, Jai," smirked Nilay. Jai's sense of humor—even his attempts at humor—was a charming quirk that infused Nilay with jollity. The boy knew he had certainly partnered with the right genie, as Jai's ingenuous nature ensured Nilay's many escapades were truly enjoyable.

The action in the palace began. Nilay watched attentively as gracious palace staff welcomed the silk merchants into the palaces to present their silken wares. The king received the first choice of silk clothing. The monarch was fashion-forward from neck to ankles, dressed in richly ornate silks intricately woven with gold threads.

"What a gentleman," commented Nilay with a hint of sarcasm. "My dad says ladies should go first."

"Shhh!" said Jai, as if he were at the movies, deeply concentrating on the action. "I'm trying to pay attention!"

Next, the queen made her choice of fine silk sarees. Princes soon arrived after dropping their fencing activities to make their selection of new silk clothes. Characteristically mild-mannered princesses squealed with delight. Their starstruck eyes glanced from one lovely new saree to the next, all attractively hung around the palace hall.

"So this is how Saurashtrians lived nearly seven hundred years ago!" said an enlightened Nilay. "This is way better than reading my favorite history books!"

"Or watching movies!" Jai added. Nilay gave Jai a knowing glance.

What took place before their eyes was a celebration of superb silk, a festival of vivid colors that thrilled the senses. In order of hierarchy, each family member was given the opportunity to buy their preferred silk garments from the Saurashtrian silk merchants.

"Does this event go on every day?" asked Nilay.

"Well, the Saurashtrian silk merchants ride up to the palace every few weeks, you know," said Jai. "And, visit after visit, the king is continually pleased."

"I would be too, if I were a king surrounded by a shower of color," said Nilay.

"Well, they didn't have showers in those days, but that's off-topic," said Jai.

Nilay rolled his eyes at Jai and said, "I'm sure the Vijayanagara royal family had plumbing of some sort."

"That is the correct answer! Now select your prize," said Jai, suddenly wearing the classic suit and yellow polka-dotted tie of a game show host.

Nilay gave Jai a friendly jab. He continued to watch ancient business dealings happen right before him.

"You know, the royal families' satisfaction with the

Saurashtrians' fine workmanship ensured enduring royal patronage," boasted Jai.

As the transaction came to an end, the king's minister approached the Saurashtrian silk merchants. He handed them a carefully rolled piece of paper bearing the imprint of the king's ring on a wax seal.

"What is this?" asked the surprised merchants.

"We have here a royal invitation from the king himself welcoming the community of Saurashtrian silk weavers and silk merchants to take up residence near the illustrious new Vijayanagara Empire capital," said the royal minister.

Privileged to serve the royal families, the humble Saurashtrian silk merchants smiled graciously. Each brought their palms together in a gesture of appreciation. The tall merchant tucked the invitation into his pocket and took it back to their community.

Jai smiled and said, "We're making progress on our hunt for the perfect red silk saree. Guess where we're headed next!"

Chapter 12

The Journey

THE KING OF THE Vijayanagara Empire was also its supreme commander, the greatest warrior of all four arms of the military. He proceeded first along the road to the new capital.

The king, wearing a yellow silk turban, rode atop his mighty elephant. Gorgeous velvet and silk cloths, richly decorated with swirling disc patterns in dizzying colors, draped over the elephant's back and fell across its sides. Just before dawn, artists had painted the elephant's face and trunk with bright pigments. The king's personal elephant's legs and the front center of its trunk were painted with the image of lotus flowers—the symbol of perfection and prosperity. Freshly assembled flower garlands and chains of pure silver ornaments hung around the animal's neck.

"Elephants in India," said Jai as Nilay watched the royal

family start their long trek, "were not only war animals. They were also revered. You see, Nilay, the Indians viewed the elephant as good luck and as a remover of obstacles!"

"I get it," replied Nilay. "The elephant symbolizes success and makes sure there are no problems on the path to the new capital!"

"You catch on quickly, my friend and master," said Jai.

"What's that in the king's hand?" asked Nilay, noticing the rod with a piercing metal tip.

"Oh, what a terrible practice!" answered Jai. "What you see is called an ankus, or elephant goad. A metal hook is attached to the end of a long stick. The tool was used by ancients to control elephants."

"How horrible! I certainly wouldn't want anyone to poke me with a metal hook," said Nilay.

"Indeed," said Jai. "A simple 'turn left' or 'turn right' is all that's necessary!"

An air of pomp and circumstance surrounded the king's procession toward the new capital. Behind the king rode the crown prince, also on a majestically decorated elephant. A body of elite generals followed the prince. Ranks of superintendents, cavalrymen and infantry strode behind.

"You know, Nilay," said Jai, "the Vijayanagara Empire is boldly equipped with nine hundred elephants, one hundred thousand infantry and twenty thousand brave cavalrymen!"

Nilay gasped in disbelief at the sheer size of the military. "It's almost impossible to believe an army can be that huge. But I believe it, because I see them right in front of me!"

"And," continued Jai, as if he were taking pleasure in throwing out factual tidbits to stun his credulous friend, "the royal army has two million soldiers, made up of musketeers, expert archers and foot soldiers."

"What an impressive force!" exclaimed Nilay, mesmerized at the magnitude of power before him.

The enormous wave of elephants, horses and foot soldiers continually kicked up a whirlwind of dust in the arid Indian climate. Behind the imposing imperial entourage followed a nimble line of Saurashtrian silk weavers and silk merchants.

The Saurashtrians clanked and clamored by on bullock carts pulled by tired oxen, camels with multiple frolicking children riding their humps and several community members casually ambling a good portion of the distance on foot.

"We're traveling with *them!*" said Jai, pointing to hundreds of Saurashtrian silk weavers, merchants and their families strolling by, cracking jokes and laughing amongst one other.

The last of them passed. A young camel strolled along with no master to guide it. "There's our ticket to the new capital!" said Jai. He ran to the camel and pulled its dangling rope harness.

"Get on!"

Nilay gleefully hopped and skipped toward the camel. The animal batted its long eyelashes while chewing on several thorny twigs. Thinking the act would be easy, Nilay attempted to hop on.

Being quite moody, the camel pushed forward before Nilay could climb aboard. Nilay fell to the ground. "Hey!" he screamed. "Come on, you rascal!"

Nilay made a second and third attempt to mount the temperamental camel. Each time, he failed. The camel looked at the frustrated Nilay out of one dainty eye. The camel nonchalantly continued eating, now chewing on dried grass.

The young boy stopped in his tracks. A bright idea popped into Nilay's head. He remembered the dates in his pockets.

He pulled out the dates. "Come hither, lovely camel!" said

Nilay, as he held out the dates in the palm of his hand. "You don't need to feed on dry twigs when juicy dates are available!"

The camel stopped chewing. It spit out the dry grasses in its mouth. The animal eyed the dates in Nilay's hand. "Come closer! Come on!" said Nilay. Slowly, the camel inched a few steps closer to Nilay.

The boy reached out and patted the camel's head. He backed away a few feet, luring the camel toward him. The camel approached, its mouth salivating for the delectable fruit.

Nilay stopped. He had coaxed the camel, which was now eating the dates out of Nilay's hands. Speaking soothing words, Nilay gently stroked the camel's head. He slowly pulled the harness down, gingerly drawing the camel downward. The animal kneeled, and Nilay climbed on.

"You made friends with the sulky camel!" shouted Jai, who had watched the whole event from afar.

"Shhh!" said Nilay. "Don't irritate him!"

Awkwardly seated and sandwiching the camel's single hump, Nilay and Jai sauntered off into the horizon. Nilay led the camel, with Jai as a rear-seat passenger.

"This promises to be a bumpy ride!" said Nilay. "But less bumpy than your piloting and landing skills!"

Jai let out a hoot and slapped his knee.

Teasing and chuckling the whole way, the two friends followed the last of the migrating Saurashtrian silk weavers and merchants to the new capital.

Chapter 13
The New Capital

THE NEW CAPITAL WAS a mere twelve miles south of the original, but traveling on the back of a sluggish animal took hours. Nilay and Jai plodded along a series of well-developed roads built by industrious kings. These intertwining roads crisscrossed the entire country. Mistakenly turning left instead of right at the fork in the road meant they would cross the borders into a completely new kingdom.

"Follow the Saurashtrians, who are following the army, who are following the king!" yelled Jai.

"I'm trying!" retorted Nilay, struggling to maneuver his camel up the hillside road.

In due course, they arrived at the northern bank of the river. Nilay, Jai and their camel ferried across the Tungabhadra River on a circular bamboo boat.

The grand Vijayanagara capital emerged in the distance. Nilay and Jai witnessed a city of forts, royal complexes, temples and memorial structures. Nilay halted the camel on the edge of the river bank in order to absorb the breathtaking magnificence before him.

Built to endure, the stone forts at the capital reached intimidating heights. Nilay was just a speck in comparison to them. Lavish temples, even from a distance, displayed architectural brilliance, such as intricately carved pillars, delicate interiors and grand-scale facades that were flanked with precisely chiseled, life-sized male and female figures. Nilay was enthralled to be surrounded by not only all this, but numerous masterfully carved soapstone sculptures that added a wealth of grandeur to the capital.

Still seated on his camel, Nilay inhaled deeply, as if to breathe in the awesomeness in front of him.

Jai, also seemingly taken by the majesty, said, "You know, this was an important city for kings for centuries!"

Nilay replied, "You mean all this glory existed before the Vijayanagara Empire ever took power?"

"Yes sir! Previous empires had built glorious monuments here. The city even served as a second royal residence once upon a time."

"Wow!" said Nilay, his eyes as big as discs.

"But, Nilay, most of the city's sixteen hundred monuments will be built by the Vijayanagara Empire's kings during their two-hundred-year reign."

Nilay got off his camel. Jai, too, hopped off the beast.

"This is the empire that will provide royal patronage for the Saurashtrian silk weavers and silk merchants for the next two centuries," said Jai. "The brook we crossed, the Tungabhadra River, is the lifeblood of this kingdom. The people here eat well and live merrily, because of the city's abundant agriculture."

"Tell me more about the awesome Vijayanagara Empire," said Nilay.

"Shall we fast forward?" asked Jai, briefly grabbing a remote control from out of the blue.

"Yes, let's roll to another historic period!" said an excited Nilay.

"Take my hand. We shall dip in the Tungabhadra River. When we emerge from the waters, we will be in the very moment when the Vijayanagara Empire was at its height!" said Jai.

Nilay's eyes became downcast and his shoulders hunched. Nilay meekly asked, "I won't drown? I mean, the river, I'm sure, can get quite deep, and with me being unable to swim, Jai, I don't know." Nilay stood frozen for a moment, anticipating being submerged in the water yet again. He'd already drowned nearly twice. The first time, his father pulled him out from the depths of Lake Ontario; the second time, Jai was there in India's ancient stepwell to lend him a hand.

"Think about it, Nilay," said Jai. "I'm learning about all the tips and tricks of being a genie; and I admit, with all the mistakes and lessons, I may end up being a world-class one at the end of it! And, you, Nilay, are learning to overcome your fears. You're safe with me, my friend and master. We also have a perfect red silk saree to get ahold of. Besides, have I ever let you down…or drown?"

Nilay imagined his loving mom, happily dancing around in a red silk saree, one he planned to give with wholehearted love. Nilay's affection for his mom emboldened him. A sense of relief overcame him, similar to that day on the beach when he was first drawn to the brass lamp. His heart filled with trust in his genie friend.

"Despite your bumpy rides, I'd say you haven't, ever!" responded Nilay with a smile.

The youth and the apprentice genie walked toward the edge of the river bank. Nilay timidly placed one foot into the cool river. Then he tightly clasped Jai's hand. Both instantly disappeared.

Just seconds later, Nilay stepped out of the river.

"I'm all wet, and...I'm alright!" said Nilay. He was drenched, from his black hair to his clothes to his gym shoes. *I can do this!* he thought. Nilay discovered plunging into the water with his genie friend was not so bad. He'd emerged just fine. The boy had a little help in the water, but that was what friends—and apprentice genies—were for.

"Well, of course! You've just taken a dip in the river with me," said Jai, also soaked and stepping out from the water.

"Oh, that's right. We've traveled through time!" said Nilay.

"Let's go sightseeing!" said Jai, pulling out a tourist hat and a camera and throwing on a boldly colored button-up Hawaiian shirt.

"I like your style!" joked Nilay. He dove into his back pocket and pulled out his damp but functional phone.

Walking along the river, they were in the imperial city's heartbeat. Nilay and Jai strolled about portions of the kingdom, which spanned sixty miles in circumference.

"This city has seven layers of fortification," said Jai.

"Seven thick walls? Wow!"

The two walked toward a construction known as the Queen's Bath. "The kings built majestic water structures, like this," said Jai.

"What's this gigantic basin used for?" asked Nilay.

"The Queen's Bath is a public bath for pilgrims and the like. Notice the artistic carving of a warrior battling a lion!" Nilay caught the striking image with his phone.

"Impressive water structures like these provide fresh water for the entire royal kingdom, starting with irrigation to the royal residences and then moving toward the suburbs and farms," said Jai.

"You can't have life without water!" said Nilay.

"That's right, my friend and master. And with a little bit of learned skill, water is nothing to be afraid of!" said Jai.

Chapter 14

An Elephant Joyride

TRAVELING INSIDE THE KINGDOM'S core, Nilay and Jai stumbled upon a massive elephant stable with eleven beautifully arched openings.

With his phone, Nilay snapped a photo of the resplendent stables fit for royalty. War elephants lazily ambled inside. Some of the majestic gray animals chewed on vegetation fed to them by their mahouts, also known as elephant trainers.

Nilay, hailing from a large city like Toronto, had never seen elephants up close. He said with joy, "This is my chance, Jai, to pet a real elephant!"

"Not to mention a royal elephant…an ancient elephant of gigantic proportions!" laughed Jai.

Nilay smiled.

"Your eyes twinkle, as if to betray a hint of mischief, my

friend," said Jai.

"Well," replied Nilay. "It would be a dream if I could ride the elephant!"

"Interesting, that's an idea," said Jai. "But, look, the elephants are tied by a rope attached to a metal hook in the huge chamber ceiling!"

Nilay scrunched his face for a second and gave a sideways glance toward Jai. Undefeated, Nilay said, "You're a genie, remember? You can do anything!"

"That's right! I'm the genie around here!" said Jai. The apprentice genie paced, scratching his little head for ideas. Thinking out loud, Jai mumbled, "I can transform into a ladder to reach the hook...or better yet, I can grow ten feet tall and access the hook...or..."

While Jai rambled, clearly mustering all the possibilities he could to reach the hook in the ceiling and free the elephant for a joy ride, Nilay screamed, "Hey, Jai! Up here!"

Nilay was seated on the back of the royal elephant, his hands waving to get Jai's attention.

The genie-in-training looked up, his jaw dropping to the floor. "How on earth did you get up there?" asked Jai.

"I found a set of stairs! They lead right up to the elephant's back! The hook was easy to untie from here. Hop on!" yelled Nilay.

Jai scuttled toward the opposite side of the chamber where the steps were conveniently positioned. He jumped up and onto the back of the swaying elephant.

Nilay gave a gentle nudge to the elephant, and it plodded out of its chamber. Once outside, the animal gained in spirit and moved faster.

"How awesome, Jai!" said Nilay as he reveled in the might and power of riding on the back of a true, ancient Indian war elephant. Nilay held tightly onto the elephant's back with his legs. With the freedom of a kite soaring in midair, he threw his arms up and let out a "Whoopeee!" His innocent laughs reached the surrounding treetops. Monkeys stopped climbing to witness the sight.

"I'd never get to ride on the back of an elephant anywhere at home! Riding the jungle roller coaster in Toronto doesn't even compare," said Nilay, his hair blowing in the wind.

"What a breathtaking experience," said Jai. "I could not have imagined this myself! Where are you leading the elephant?"

"I'm not!" said a jubilant Nilay. "I would never poke this awesome animal with a metal hook just to show him the way! He knows the land, and he's going wherever he wants. It's too cool for words!"

The elephant picked up speed. Within earshot, one of the mahouts screamed. Nilay looked back. The elephant trainer was running behind them, his arms flailing.

"Uh-oh," said Nilay. "We've got company! I think he wants his elephant back!"

Nilay spoke a few words into the elephant's ear and the animal lunged forward at twice his usual speed.

"The elephant trainer looks mad, and he's still behind us!" said Jai.

"No problem," said Nilay. He was determined to evade the chasing mahout.

A throng of people, minding their daily routines, were just ahead. Men and women in the crowd saw the oncoming elephant and screamed in alarm. The people scattered, making a clear path for the elephant to speed through.

Jai pulled a bullhorn from his pockets and spoke into it with the confidence of a circus ringmaster. "Step aside, ladies and gents! A two-person parade is coming through! I'd sell tickets, but this is a lightning-fast show!"

The riding duo swiftly passed through the village without harm. They eased into a grassy clearing surrounded by rows of trees that screened the boy from the elephant handler. The animal slowed down. Nilay stroked the elephant's head and said, "You look tired, good boy!" Here, the elephant kneeled and allowed Nilay and Jai to leap off his back.

Wiping sweat from his forehead, Nilay heaved, "Whoa! That was a once-in-a-lifetime experience!"

"And we weren't even in battle!" retorted Jai. "The mahout will find his elephant drinking from the nearby pond and will return him safe and sound to the stable."

Nilay grabbed his phone from his pocket and snapped a photo of the resting elephant. He sat down beside the war elephant, leaning his back against the grand animal.

"I will remember this forever," said Nilay as a dreamy smile spread across his face. He closed his eyes and relished his experience of joyriding on the back of a genuine, ancient Indian war elephant.

Nilay's bliss was interrupted. The mahout's screams were getting closer. "Time to go!" said Nilay. The young boy gently patted the elephant farewell. Nilay and his genie companion ran off, leaving the war elephant with a few more minutes of pure freedom.

Into the thickets scurried Nilay and Jai.

"Shall we continue our sightseeing?" asked Jai.

"The elephant ride was a wild adventure. It will stick with me! Still, let us explore," replied Nilay. His youthful energy was perfectly suited for countless exploits.

They passed a council hall, known as the Lotus Mahal, showing off stunning architectural elements. It was located in the royal center.

"The Lotus Mahal fails to bear any inscriptions," said Jai. "So no one knows for sure what it was used for."

"A centuries' long mystery," said Nilay, getting a snapshot, "that deserves to be preserved in a photo!" They both continued their tour around the ancient kingdom.

Nilay stopped before a skyscraper-like monument, standing sixteen feet high.

"This is known as the King's Balance," said Jai. "The king sits on one end of the balance, and his ministers place gold, silvers and jewels on the other end of the balance. When the weight of gems is equal to or more than the king's weight, he gives the treasures to the priests!"

Nilay hopped onto the balance. With nothing on the opposite tray, Nilay's side of the balance heaved to the ground. Jai jumped onto the empty tray. Nilay flew into the air.

"I didn't know you were that heavy!" screamed Nilay, laughing and soaring upward.

"Even genies-in-training have a thing or two up their sleeves!"

Nilay fell lightly into a thick bush. Unscathed, he got up to join Jai.

"Traders from Portugal and Persia say the city of Vijayanagara is among the most beautiful!" said Jai with a sparkle.

"This city is amazing!" said Nilay.

Nilay and Jai walked toward the outer layers of the kingdom, filled with craftspeople and farmers.

"And this," said Jai, his voice exuding confidence, "is where the royal Saurashtrian silk weavers and silk merchants live and work."

Nilay didn't know exactly how, but he knew this was the place where he would get ahold of the perfect red silk saree.

Chapter 15
The Hero

IT WAS A LAZY day. Nilay and Jai sauntered near a stream just bordering the Saurashtrian silk weavers' and merchants' residences. Distant sounds of children frolicking in the fields echoed through the quiet atmosphere. The picturesque setting encouraged a bit of rest and relaxation.

"The sun is beating down unusually hot today," said Jai. They ambled toward a tree with its outstretched branches offering generous shade. "I'll have a nice nap right here," said Jai, and he climbed up the thick trunk. Getting comfy, Jai laid down his head and immediately started snoring.

Nilay said, "You get some rest, Jai." The young boy sat in the shade under the tree by the stream as his genie friend nestled in the cool treetops.

A light splashing broke the stillness. Undisturbed, Nilay

picked up a stick and poked it in the dirt. Fiddling with the broken branch, he imagined he was a soldier, and his stick a sword. "Take that! And that!" he shouted, plunging the branch into an imaginary enemy.

The splashing sound of water grew louder. Nilay followed the sound with his gaze. A few yards away, the sound of splashing united with the sight of splashing water.

What in the world is that? A stream creature? The likes of the Loch Ness monster here in ancient India? wondered Nilay. With the curiosity of a youth, he stumbled through the parched grasses toward the splashing.

In clear view, a little girl was being swallowed up by the stream's waters. She scarcely screamed, as most of her energy was directed toward her efforts to keep herself from drowning.

Nilay yelled, "Hey! Hey!" With his stick in hand, he rushed toward the edge of the stream. The water's depth frightened him a little. This was Nilay's moment. He had a choice. His could let his fear of the water stifle his courage. Or, he could let bravery triumph. Nilay's decision was instant and instinctive. He did not even need to think this through.

With one hand grasping the stick, he extended his arm so the girl could clutch the branch. The little girl tried to reach for it, but she was too far out in the stream.

Nilay, still afraid at the depth of the stream, forced his courage to prevail. He slowly waded in as far as he could, making sure his feet continued to touch the bed of the stream. Moving closer to the little girl, he was determined to keep his head above the water. He did not know how to swim, but he knew he was in a position to save a life.

Jai's snoring was louder than ever. The sounds of voices in the distance became clearer, as a few onlookers took notice of the struggle happening at the stream.

"Look!" said a group of Saurashtrians, still quite a distance away. They pointed toward Nilay and the little girl, who was plunging underneath the waters of the stream fast. Her arms flapped. She spat out the water, trying with all her life to stay afloat.

Nilay, filled with fear, could go no further without risking his own life. If he drowned, so would she.

With the branch still in hand, he gave one more giant heave, pushing the stick toward the girl. The onlookers were running down the hill toward the stream.

The girl's head disappeared under the water. Within the next second, she courageously re-emerged and made a grab for Nilay's stick. This time, she got a hold of it. With concentrated effort, Nilay, his nose barely above the surface of the water, slowly pulled the nearly drowning girl toward him and onto dry ground.

Exhausted by the fight for her life, the little girl collapsed onto the grass. A Saurashtrian woman burst through the throng and ran down the hill, panicking. She embraced the child, tears streaming down her face. The girl coughed up water. She was breathing.

Nilay, fatigued by the event, crawled away from the creek and lay in the shade beneath the tree. Jai's snoring was louder than ever.

The crowd of Saurashtrians had gathered. They circled Nilay and talked amongst one other, saying, "He saved her! This young boy risked his life to rescue little Ashi!"

Others clamored, "The current could have swept them both away!"

Slightly shaking with a tinge of lingering fear, Nilay rested his mind and body under the very spot he had played combat with an invisible enemy just moments before. In a beautiful way, he had conquered another invisible enemy—his fear.

Within the hour, news of Nilay's heroic efforts reached the king's ears. The monarch commanded that Nilay stand before him in the palace.

A gathering of Saurashtrians approached Nilay under the tree. They told the boy the king wanted to see him.

Nilay, by this time, had restored his strength and gotten his wits back. "Uh, whatever for?"

The Saurashtrian silk weavers and silk merchants responded by throwing Nilay onto their shoulders and walking toward the royal center. All the while, they chanted, "Hero! Hero!" At the thunderous praises, Jai startled and woke up.

"What's going on?" Jai glanced around. The crowd of the kingdom's citizens ushered Nilay away. "Wait up for me! Nilay!" Jai jumped down from his perch on the tree and scrambled behind the group of Saurashtrians transporting Nilay to the palace.

At the ornate royal gates, the Saurashtrians put Nilay down and cheered. They yelled, "Here is the hero who saved Ashi!" Palace guards opened the gates and let Nilay in.

Nilay walked inside, in awe of the grandeur, the enormous wealth and the indisputable power surrounding him. His walk toward the king seemed to take eons as he passed rows and rows of finely carved pillars painted in metallic gold sheens. Each column supported beautiful fluted arches showing off symmetrical perfection. In the corner of Nilay's eye, exquisitely decorated vases of gigantic proportions sparkled. He imagined he could easily fit inside any one of these many lacquered vases lining the hall. Looking up, even the lavishly painted palace ceilings appeared to him to be a mile high.

Resplendence saturated the palace from top to bottom. Even though the palace had a venerable place in recorded history, to Nilay, it was a unique, fantastical atmosphere right out of a story book.

At last, Nilay approached the throne room. There, the king, seated on a gilded throne, said in a grandfatherly voice, "Welcome, my child. Come closer."

Nilay took a few steps toward the royal monarch, the ruler of all south India, and stood trembling before him.

Chapter 16
The Gift

"WORD HAS REACHED ME that you risked your life to save a small child from drowning," said the king.

The monarch was seated on a lavish golden throne upholstered in rich, red velvet and studded with an assortment of colorful, glistening gems. Hanging directly above the king's throne was a huge, majestic parasol. Fresh flower garlands decorated the perimeter of the throne and released the lovely fragrance of jasmine flowers.

The throne room exuded a welcoming energy. The interior atmosphere was cool in comparison to the unbearable heat outside. Contributing to the throne room's comfort were two royal staff who steadily fanned the royal monarch. The constant breeze swept through the entirety of the area.

Nilay stuttered, "Y-ye-yes, Your Majesty." Swirling inside

his mind was the thought that he was actually speaking with the celebrated king of the incredible Vijayanagara Empire, an empire powerful and distinguished enough to be magnanimously featured in every written history of Indian civilization.

"What's your name?" asked the imperial ruler.

"Ni...Nilay," the boy replied.

"Where are you from?" asked the curious king.

"I...I'm from Toronto, Canada, Your Majesty," said Nilay. His knees trembled and almost gave out. With effort, he held himself together. Naturally, Nilay had never been in the presence of historical greatness, let alone one of such awe-inspiring magnitude.

The king scratched his chin at the mention of the unfamiliar country. "Hmmm, I see. That must be a very faraway land."

"Yes, Your Majesty. It is," said Nilay, still slightly stammering but recovering. With the monarch's gracious treatment, Nilay's shoulders gradually relaxed and his knees stopped knocking.

"Well, for your bravery, I want to reward you, child," said the dignified king. He motioned for his palace staff to approach. Their arms were filled with silken cloths.

The king, valuing compassion and honor, saw both characteristics in the young Nilay. "Take these silken cloths, personally woven by the royal silk weavers of Saurashtra."

An order is an order, thought Nilay. Saving a helpless girl when he had the chance was nothing but a humane duty, one that required no repayment. Standing there, he felt he had no choice but to accept the king's generosity.

The ruler placed the silken goods into Nilay's outstretched arms. "I am presenting you with five silk sarees, five silk salwar kameez and five silk turbans," said the king.

Nilay toppled under the sheer weight of the silks. "Thank you, Your Majesty!"

"Now go, my child. May you always be honorable," said the king and dismissed Nilay.

Carrying the load of silks was a challenge. Nilay stumbled a bit but managed to walk to the edge of the palace gates without dropping a single silk cloth.

Waiting outside, Jai screamed, "Nilay! Over here!"

Nilay, his bright eyes peering from just above the top of the silk pile, moved toward Jai. The crowd yelled, "Hooray!" when Nilay made his reappearance after speaking with the king.

Noticing Nilay's efforts to keep his gifts from dropping to the ground, members of the crowd pulled up a wooden cart. They piled the numerous silks into the cart and put Nilay onto it just the same. Jai followed with the crowd as they guided the cart back to the village on the outskirts of the kingdom.

During the whole ride, Nilay sat pondering his royal gifts. There were so many! He knew what he would do with the silks.

As soon as the cart reached the outer suburbs, Nilay got off, his silk cloths in his arms.

"My, oh my!" said Jai. "You've caught quite a load! Sarees and turbans of all the colors of the rainbow! Green, red, blue, purple! What a spectacle! They are shimmering like diamonds. What incredible riches! Hmm, let's see…in today's dollars, you could buy a crystal-studded toy ship or a giant, inflatable water slide for endless summertime fun or…"

"Well, they are not all meant for me," Nilay replied.

"Whatever do you mean?" asked the surprised Jai. "The king gave them to you!"

"You'll see," said Nilay.

Just then, Nilay passed an elderly man seated on the ground. He wore nothing but a tattered cloth and carried a simple, worn staff. His head sweltered under the sun's rays.

Nilay pulled a silk salwar kameez and silk turban from his load, smiled and said, "Here you are, sir. New silk clothes! And a silk turban to keep your head cool!" The old man gave a toothless grin. He held out his arms and happily accepted Nilay's gift.

"That's quite a gesture," said Jai.

"They need these clothes more than I do," replied Nilay as they continued walking down the village streets.

He came across a middle-aged man slumped on the ground and wearing an old dhoti with holes in it. Nilay presented this man with new silken clothes. The man smiled faintly, barely able to acknowledge the bigheartedness of the tender boy.

Then Nilay approached a tired woman, her face weathered by a lifetime of struggle. She wore a threadbare, faded cotton saree. She sat at the edge of a beaten porch with a crying, hungry baby in her arms. "Take this saree, good ma'am," said Nilay, laying the new silk at her bare, dust-covered feet.

Nilay continued this way, gifting the needy men and women of the kingdom with royally produced turbans, salwar kameez and sarees—until he was almost out of the silks.

"There's only one I'm going to keep, for now," said Nilay to his genie friend.

"Huh? And which one is that?"

"This one, this most perfect red silk saree in the world," said an exuberant Nilay, his hands pressing the silk against his smiling cheek.

Chapter 17
The Empire's Fall

NILAY SHARED HIS SPIRIT of fulfillment with his genie friend. Nilay had gotten his wish and more. He could believe in himself now. After all, his courage had overpowered his fear. His newfound confidence had not only saved a young life but resulted in him being presented with the most perfect red silk saree for his beloved mom's birthday.

BOOM! The sound of a cannon pierced the thick air, like a needle through a thin fabric quilt.

Suddenly, the kingdom's residents screamed, "The empire is under attack!" Masses of people scattered, running chaotically throughout the kingdom to escape the rapid sequence of cannon fire.

"Oh, no!" shouted Nilay, shuddering. The sky grew gray with an avalanche of smoke from the blazing fires that fast destroyed the palaces, the royal structures and the citizens' homes.

"It must be the invaders from the north," yelled Jai. The genie-in-training whipped out an encyclopedia, scanned the entries with lightning-fast swiftness and exclaimed, "It's written right here. The five sultanates have formed an alliance, and now they are attempting to defeat the king of Vijayanagara!"

Jai hurled the book out of hands, and the two frantically scrambled left and right, not sure which way to go.

"Follow the Saurashtrian silk weavers!" shouted Jai, pointing to rushing passersby.

"Where are they going?" asked Nilay, running toward the groups of townsfolk embarking on a new migration. He held the precious red silk saree close to his chest even as he trekked toward the chaotic migrators.

Between the razing cannon shots, the burning monuments and the swarm of terrified people clamoring for safety, Jai screamed, "They're heading south!"

Nilay and Jai crawled into the back of a moving, wheeled cart pushing forward on the roads leading out of the devastated kingdom. They took cover under a muslin cloth.

Whispering, Jai said, "Nilay, this is the last of the Saurashtrian migrations! The first group will move into a nearby town called Salem. A second group of silk weavers and merchants will make their home in the more southern city of Thanjavur. The final group of Saurashtrian migrators will settle in the southernmost city of Madurai."

The wooden cart moved steadily onward. Soon, the deafening roar of cannon fire subsided. Nilay and Jai were out of harm's way.

"I think we're safe now," said Jai quietly.

"What happened to the empire?" asked a shaking Nilay.

"The empire did not stand a chance," replied Jai. His voice was marked with sadness. "The Vijayanagara Empire was one of the largest and wealthiest kingdoms India has ever known. The arts and literature flourished there, like springtime grasses in April."

It was certain. Over a series of battle defeats, the last of the Vijayanagara Empire finally fell. It was the year 1565 CE.

The quiet of the south displaced the noise of the sudden invasion. Bit by bit, Nilay and Jai made progress along the path of safety with the Saurashtrian silk weavers and merchants.

The tenseness in Nilay's chest gradually disappeared as he and his genie companion rode into calmer territories. He looked at the red silk saree in his hands.

"My wish is granted!" He gurgled with boyish happiness.

In an optimistic tone, Jai said, "Now, my wish is to get us back! I'm sure I can figure it out!"

"Our adventure is almost over," said Nilay, sadly. He perked up and said, "But let's see what the Saurashtrian silk weavers and silk merchants do in their new land!"

"Will do!" Jai beamed.

They both sat comfortably in the back of the wooden cart, relaxing and taking in the new sights and sounds of the exotic south.

The Saurashtrians' journey was as interesting as their silks were colorful. Their route to the south meant they'd pass through many populated areas. Traveling through India's southern regions, the Saurashtrians absorbed the flavors of the local peoples' cultures and languages.

"It's been a long journey, my friend and master!" said Jai.

"It sure has! I'd never trade all the excitement from this adventure for anything," replied Nilay. "I learned so much, firsthand. I overcame my fear of water, and I am ready for swim lessons when I get home. Even better, in the end, I got the perfect birthday present for my mom!"

"I learned so much, too. Being a genie does seem to take some skill," said Jai. "Given that, I think I'll peel back wish granting just a teensy bit."

"Why?" countered Nilay. "I think your genie skills are top-notch!"

Jai sighed. "Well, you know, I could use a lesson or two from my dad. He's the pro! The expert! The finest genie I've ever known! And I can't wait to get back to relish his splendid lunch spread. I can smell it now: fresh kabobs, tantalizing curries..."

"Aw, shucks, Jai! I'm starting to feel hungry, too!"

With the red silk saree hanging over one arm, Nilay wrapped his other arm around Jai's shoulder. Jai did the same. Intertwined as forever friends, the two smiling youths leaped off the cart and walked into a bustling Indian marketplace.

Chapter 18

The Return Home

SETTLING IN SMALL TOWNS, like Salem, and large metropolises, like Thanjavur and Madurai, the Saurashtrians' expeditions finally ended in India's deep south.

Nevertheless, a new beginning took place.

"What's that delicious smell?" asked Nilay. He and Jai both strolled Salem's gravelly roads. The aromas of lemon rice and fried dosai wafted through the streets.

"You must really have an appetite," joked Jai.

"I do! Well, you didn't say, Jai. Who rules over India's south now?" asked Nilay.

"The new kings of the Nayak dynasty wield their powers in the south," answered Jai.

"Are these new kings as noble as the Vijayanagara kings?" asked Nilay.

"The new rulers are lifelong patrons of the arts. It's good to know the Nayak kings equally welcomed the renowned Saurashtrian saree artisans. The silk weavers were so valued, they were even invited to make their homes near the Nayak's Thirumalai Nayakkar Palace."

"Wow!" responded Nilay.

"Indeed, the Saurashtrian silk weavers and silk merchants continued in prestige and experienced a wealth of happiness for centuries. They enjoyed long-term prosperity in the hospitable arms of many kings," said Jai.

A Saurashtrian passerby accidentally bumped into Nilay. He uttered a few words and politely moved on.

"What'd he say?" asked Nilay to his well-versed genie companion. "His language is different from what we've heard all along."

"It's the unique language of the Saurashtrians!" replied Jai.

"Oh, I see. They developed their own language! But how?" asked Nilay with deep-seated curiosity.

"Well, you know, being in a new land, the Saurashtrians fused the original languages of Gujarat with the languages of the people with whom they interacted throughout their migratory journeys. The melodious result was a fusion of the Indo-Aryan language of Gujarati and the Dravidian languages of Tamil and Telugu."

"When I get back home, I'm going to look up the Saurashtrian alphabet online and learn to speak the language!" said Nilay.

"Well, that would be fruitless, my friend and master."

"Huh? Why is that?"

"See, without a written script, countless variations of the Saurashtra language exist, leading to varying dialects. The Saurashtrians speak different dialects in India's northern and southern parts of the state of Tamil Nadu," said Jai.

"So, how do they communicate with one other?"

"The Saurashtrians still speak Saurashtra at home, and are bilingual in both Tamil and Telugu," answered Jai.

Showing off his worldly knowledge, Jai continued, "The word 'Saurashtra' literally translates into 'good country'. Saurashtrians find home wherever they go. In the twenty-first century, the descendants of the ancient silk weavers and silk merchants are found all over the globe, from Europe to America to Australia."

"And Canada!" contributed Nilay.

"Indeed," said Jai.

"What about in India?" asked Nilay.

"You know, Saurashtrians also continue to live in closely knit communities in southern India—nearly one thousand years after their very first southbound migration. Even today, thirty thousand silk weavers are found near Madurai, weaving silk sarees, silk turbans and silk salwar kameez fit for kings," said Jai, his chest puffed up.

Nilay glanced down at the red silk saree carefully tucked in his arms. The saree was beautifully woven, its golden threads dancing in the light of the sun.

"That is the loveliest of sarees, and it's far from an ordinary work of art," said Jai. "The saree was made with heart." Jai continued, "People who wear the Saurashtrians' silks are transformed. Wrapped in joy, men and women experience incredible feelings of luxury while wearing the beautiful silk cloth. Why? Because each silk saree produced by the Saurashtrian silk weavers gets its miraculous beginnings at the hand looms, still used today in India by these munificent groups of exceptionally talented artisans."

"My mom will absolutely love this saree on her birthday,"

said Nilay joyfully. "I can't wait to give it to her."

Beaming with pride, Nilay remarked, "You granted my wish, and added a hefty dose of surprises in the process!"

"Aw, shucks, Nilay," said Jai, blushing like a blooming rose. "It was nothing!"

Nilay stood before Jai as a young boy who had seen ancient kingdoms rise and powerful empires fall, and as a youth who had witnessed the people dedicated to time-honored artistic traditions remain as strong as they were a millennium ago.

"Jai, I have to shake your hand."

"Isn't that how we got into this whole quest in the first place?" quipped Jai with a gleam in his eye.

"And there's no adventure better than this one!"

Clutching the saree, Nilay offered his free hand to Jai. The apprentice genie, with an ear-to-ear smile, grasped his hand firmly and shook it.

Instantly, they both vanished.

Chapter 19

Back in Canada

NILAY FOUND HIMSELF STANDING on a flat rock. Lake Ontario's waves had smoothed the rock's surface. "Perfect landing!" Nilay thought aloud. He glanced around. On his arm hung the beautiful red silk saree, but Jai was nowhere in sight.

He sniffed the air. The delicious aroma of fried samosas wafted into Nilay's nostrils. He looked down. The brass lamp rested between a few rocks. A squeaky voice drew Nilay toward the delicate object. The familiar voice came from inside the lamp: "Delish, Dad! You make the most awesome samosas!"

Nilay smiled knowingly.

The lamp suddenly flitted and flipped and fell into the water. He watched the lamp float farther away in the lake until it disappeared. "Until we meet again, my friend!" said Nilay with a tender heart.

Nilay held on to the saree. He carefully crossed the rocks and ran back to his mom and dad, who were sitting on the other side of the beach.

"Mom! Dad!" yelled Nilay.

"You disappeared like a ghost these past ten minutes, Nilay! Your dad and I were looking all over Bluffers Park Beach for you. Lunch is almost ready," Nilay's mom said with a sigh of relief.

"Ah, Mom, don't worry! I was on the other side of the beach by the rocks!" the youth replied.

The beach at Toronto's Bluffers Park featured dramatic steep bluffs against the pillow-soft sands. Crowds of people and families took advantage of the cool lakefront breeze, lay on the popular beach, bicycled along its shoreline and frolicked in its waters a safe distance from the rocks.

"What's that hanging on your arm, sweetheart?" asked Nilay's mom.

"Mom, this is for you! It's your birthday present! Happy birthday!" said Nilay.

"Darling, all you need to do is smile and you light up my heart." She took the saree and held the soft silk cloth. Nilay's dad ruffled his son's hair.

Nilay's mom gently wrapped the luxurious silk saree around her arm. "Why, Nilay, this is the most perfect red silk saree I've ever seen!" She smiled. Her face brightened.

"I knew you'd love it, Mom!"

"Where on earth did you get such a gorgeous piece of art?" she asked with an expression of bewilderment.

"From the Saurashtrian royal weavers! See, I went on this great adventure to India. I traveled back in time with a real genie..." said Nilay, starting to tell his story.

"Dear child, your imagination has the best of you!"

His dad chimed in, "You know, hon, boys will be boys! And Nilay, you're my number one dreamer!"

"No, look, Mom and Dad! I have pictures!" Nilay pulled out his phone and showed them the photos he took of the King's Balance and the elephant stable from a time long past.

"Did you pull up these photos online? Have you been playing with Photoshop, dear boy? Your Photoshop skills are quite impressive, I do have to say. But, my goodness, Nilay!" said his mom.

"Mom, really, it all started on the other side of the beach..." said Nilay. He told his mom and dad about his entire journey.

"Well, as you say, darling," she said. "Dad is ready to unpack our picnic lunch. Let's chow down!"

The young boy followed his mom, and they walked toward the picnic tables. Dad set out a marvelous spread of samosas, fried breads and a plate of sweet dates.

"Mom, Dad, I'm also ready for swim lessons," said Nilay.

"What great news! You've been jittery around water for a while now. I don't know what changed your mind, dear, but I am glad you did," said his mom. "Once you get comfortable in the water, we can all go for fun weekend swims together!"

His dad said, "I'm proud of you, son, for being bigger than your fears."

Nilay took one glance back at the lake. He scurried a few steps toward the edge of the beach. Then, as carefree as a joyful child, he hopped and skipped toward his family and the waiting lunch.

Against the horizon, the lamp briefly reappeared along the surface of the lake. Through its curled tip, the lamp shot a stream of water into the sunlit sky. Within the droplets of water, a rainbow appeared for just a few moments, like a colorful half halo over the lamp. With the falling of the precipitation, the brass lamp leaped, did a quick, happy spin and disappeared once more beneath the water.

Chronology and Note Regarding Real Historical Events

Apart from flying carpets and apprentice genies granting wishes for the first time, several historical events regarding the close-knit community of Saurashtrians actually took place. The real-life historic moments and the dates they occurred are broken down here:

322 BCE – Saurashtra is a kingdom of its own, ruled over by India's Maurya Empire. Saurashtra is located in present-day Gujarat in northwest India. The Arabian Sea borders Saurashtra to the southwest.

268 BCE – Ashoka the Great, of the Maurya Empire, governs over Saurashtra.

320 CE – The Gupta Empire rules from northern India to central India and part of the country's south. Saurashtrian silk weavers and silk merchants live in the kingdom as a peace-loving community, practicing their silk weaving artistry for centuries to come. The Gupta era is recognized as India's "Golden Age."

1027 CE – Turkish ruler Mahmud Ghazni invades northwest India, including the Saurashtra region. The 1027 CE raid is the last and biggest of his seventeen invasions of

India. Ghazni plunders India's Somnath Temple, located along the Saurashtrian coast, of its vast riches. Many Saurashtrians migrate southward, into Maharashtra, to escape from Ghazni's repeated attacks. For several more centuries, the Saurashtrian silk weavers and silk merchants practice their artistry in this new and more peaceful land.

1336 CE – The Vijayanagara Empire is formed. The empire, at its height, is the wealthiest and largest empire of its time in the world. The Vijayanagara kings and the families are dedicated patrons of the Saurashtrian silk weavers' and silk merchants' arts. When they shift their capital to a more secure location, the kings invite the Saurashtrian silk weavers and silk merchants to take up residence in their expanded kingdom. In these flourishing times, the Saurashtrian artisans become the trusted royal weavers.

1565 CE – The Vijayanagara Empire falls after repeated military defeats. The new Nayak kings welcome the Saurashtrian silk weavers and silk merchants into their circle of royal artisans. The new kingship rules over southern cities like Madurai. In this city, the kings build a grand palace known as the Thirumalai Nayak Palace, a masterful work of architecture that can be visited even today. The largest group of Saurashtrians migrate as far south as Madurai, taking up residence near the Nayaks' majestic palace as the royal weavers. Two smaller groups of Saurashtrian silk weavers and silk merchants settle in Salem and Thanjavur, also governed by the Nayak kings.

1948 CE – After India's independence from the British government, Saurashtra merges with 217 princely states and is given the new moniker Saurashtra State. The renamed state includes 222 local princes.

1956 CE – Saurashtra State merges into Bombay State.

1960 CE – The Saurashtra region becomes a part of the state of Gujarat.

Today – In south India, the contemporary Saurashtrian community thrives. Saurashtrian silk weavers still practice their ancient silk weaving artistic traditions, especially in the Indian state of Tamil Nadu, where the population of Saurashtrians is strong.

In the present day, many worldly Saurashtrians, having taken up various intellectual professions, emigrate out of India and spread across the globe. Saurashtrians make their homes in Australia, England, Canada, the United States and a multitude of other nations.

Acknowledgements

I had the joyous experience of working with many exceptional people while publishing *Nilay's Wish*. Many thanks to my editor Alexandra Ott and proofreader Erin Black for their invaluable observations and tweaks. Much gratitude to illustrator Akos Horvath for brilliantly bringing to vivid life my story's characters and infusing the illustrations with exuberance, historical realism and flair. Heartfelt cheers to my family, who somehow never run out of patience.